When the Street Lights Come On

Terry –
  I hope you enjoy reading
the stories of <u>my</u> childhood
and know that someone
is waiting to hear <u>yours</u>.

  Best Wishes,

  Jim McMullen
  2/9/04

Published by
James A. McMullen Publishing
775 Empress Ave, Camarillo, CA 93010

Cover Design by Annie Ludes

First Edition
ISBN 0-9721942-0-7

The stories contained in this book come
from real people and places. The intent,
when mentioning names, was to be
historically accurate without being
hurtful. If anyone mentioned in this work
takes offense to the words used to
describe them or situations that involved
them, I apologize.

"A life is not important except in the impact it has on other lives."

Jackie Robinson

"When a grandparent dies, a library burns down."

Alex Haley

Introduction

Stories define lives. They lay sheltered deep within the brain obscured only by the element of time. When one dies so die the stories, and the documentation needed to preserve a memory vanishes.

Contained in stories are feelings — emotions created by circumstances often beyond our control. Feelings are both unique and universal at the same time. Unique because each person reacts to experiences differently and universal because there are only so many kinds of feelings that human beings can experience.

Feelings transcend time. A feeling created a generation ago, as a reaction to a situation or event, can be experienced by someone today if similar conditions exist. Similar experiences will elicit similar feelings. Stories serve as vehicles to transport the feelings. They define who we are and make each of us unique.

This is the story of my childhood. It takes place between 1956 and 1963 in a small city in Southern California. It was a time before video games and microwave ovens, before solar energy and compact discs. It was a time when television pictures were in black and white and computers were just being developed. No one had yet seen, much less actually used, a calculator or digital watch.

Life was somewhat different for kids then — a little slower and a lot less complicated — but the fundamental reactions to events were the same. They remain constant over time.

The first time I kissed a girl or the most embarrassing moment of my life — two entirely different events I assure you — both have associated feelings that transcend time. The feelings I experienced as a kid can be mirrored by someone experiencing the same events today.

On September 11, 1994, exactly 7 years before the tragic events in New York, Cody James Arthur

McMullen was born. He weighed 5 lbs. 11 ounces, blond hair, blue eyes, with all his toes and fingers in their proper places. As I peered through the window into the nursery at my first grandchild I was overwhelmed. His tiny body tucked securely under a blue trimmed blanket meant now there was a complete generation between us. I decided at that exact moment, to build a bridge to span the newly created generation gap.

My plan was simple. The construction material would primarily be words. I'd write about the things I experienced as a kid growing up and offer them to Cody. As he read the words I used to describe my life experiences, he'd be uncovering the feelings those experiences created for me. Then maybe he'd recognize the same feelings as he journeyed through his life. If so, a connection would be forged between my life then and his life now. The resulting connection would be our bond — a bond of shared feelings, and the bridge would be complete.

When I was a kid, we'd play outside during the summer until dark. Before night actually fell Mom would issue the order, "Come home when the street lights come on." So the street lights became the universal signal that meant it was time to go home.

This book is about going home, about returning to a familiar place to retrieve some feelings. Once found, I'll transport these feelings through time using words as a vehicle. Cody can then sift through them and hopefully discover something magical — similar experiences, same feelings, and the resulting connection.

I hope you enjoy reading these stories, all of which are true, and that you'll discover some feelings you can relate to as well. It's the sharing of feelings that makes life so special and creates the bonds between us.

It's getting dark and the street lights are about to come on. It's time to head for home...

James A. McMullen

THE CONTEST

I have twin sisters. *I'm* not a twin, my sisters are. I'm actually a year older than they are. Can you imagine my mom? When I was eighteen months old she had two six month old girls to contend with. Ever try carrying around three little kids at once? You can see why at eight months old I learned to walk, I saw what was coming and did something about it!

My sisters were as different as night and day. They looked alike but that's where it ended. Sandy, the younger by half an hour, was sweet, dainty, and loved dolls and playing house. Charlene preferred bicycles, baseball, and climbing trees. I spent most of my childhood with Char. I'm not sure what Sandy did or where she did it, but I suppose whatever it was, she was happy doing it.

Char was my best friend. The main reason was that she was really good at everything. When the guys in the neighborhood got together for a game of touch football in the street we'd choose up sides. Since Char was always at my side she'd be part of the game as well. Inevitably, she'd be picked before half of the other boys. This fact didn't exactly boost the pride of those picked after her but, she was faster and could throw and catch better than most of the guys, so that was that. No matter what we did or where we went Char and I were a great team together.

It was the start of summer, just after I finished fifth grade, that the local TG &Y — a dime store — held a model building contest for boys and girls eight to twelve years old. Char and I were always eager to try something new, so the following Saturday, we jumped on our bikes and headed down to get the details.

From across the parking lot we could see a huge banner hanging above the window. "The Master Model Builder's Contest" it proclaimed sponsored by Revell, a popular model manufacturer. As I stared at the banner it occurred to me that this was something I had been preparing for all my life. Over the last couple of years I'd made a lot of models and I liked to think I learned something about the process along the way. "Why don't we enter?" I said to Char. It was obvious from the look on her face that she wasn't as excited about this as I was which was understandable; she hadn't ever made a model before. But what she lacked in enthusiasm, she made up for with cooperation. Being the good sport she was, she agreed to give it a try.

We entered the store and headed for the aisle where the modeling supplies were located. My imagination soared as everything needed to build a model was spread out before us: hundreds of kits to choose from, paint, brushes, glue, X-acto knives, and an assortment of decals.

These items fueled my imagination and after several minutes I had decided. A bi-plane from WW II caught my eye. It was equipped with fully functional landing gear, wings with moving stabilizers, and a propeller made of real wood. It contained more pieces than any model I'd ever attempted before. I knew this because a serial number appeared on the end of every model box which was actually a secret code. This code represented the number of pieces in the kit — the more pieces — the more difficult the task. It was exactly the kind of model that would take me to the winner's circle.

I made a mental shopping list of the items required and estimated I would need $5, a ten-week advance on my allowance. I had to promise to work around the house for as long as necessary before mom agreed to advance the necessary funds.

The next day Char and I went back to the store to make our purchases. There it was, the WW II bi-plane, perched on the top shelf where the expensive models were always kept. I reached for it and cradled it between my hands. I felt confident about this selection and the challenge that lay ahead of me. "I'll be over looking at the paint," I said to Char, who still hadn't made up her mind about which kit to buy. "I'll meet you up front at the register," and away I went.

A few minutes later, we were standing at the check-out. I placed the box containing the bi-plane in front of the checker, in addition to three bottles of paint, a brush, a bottle of thinner, and a tube of glue. "What'd you get Char?" I asked. "A sea plane," she responded.

The first thing I noticed about her selection, as it lay on the belt before the checker, was that it was little, maybe 15 or 20 pieces at most. It was going to be extremely easy to build. " Not a good choice to win a contest", I thought to myself. The next observation I made was that she was buying just the model and a tube of glue. Apparently she *wasn't* going to paint it. "Big mistake," I thought, because the picture on the box showed an *orange* sea plane! This was the type of model that cried out to be painted. But she had her own ideas and I had mine. We finished paying for the projects, jumped on our bikes, and rode home. The possibility of winning the contest now drove me. I couldn't wait to get started.

That night I read the instructions and made sure all the pieces were accounted for. I studied the sequence of events so I understood everything before I began in earnest. I had a week to build my plane and I intended to dedicate every available minute to making it perfect.

I began work the next morning. As I snapped each part from its plastic stem, I checked and double checked the instructions before applying the glue and attaching the pieces. Only the minimum amount of adhesive would be used throughout the process. There was no room for error.

I repeated this ritual daily and after each step was completed I carefully re-examined my efforts. My creation was beginning to take shape. At the conclusion of each day's work I carefully placed the work-in-progress on the top shelf in my closet, away from any danger.

At the end of the week the tedious process was finished. The fruit of my labor had ripened before my very eyes. Lying before me was an *exact* replica of the bi-plane pictured on the box. The landing gear had wheels that rolled, stabilizers on the wings could be moved to several positions, and the wooden propeller rotated with the flick of a finger. Even the paint had dried to the exact colors. It was stunning but more importantly this plane was ready for combat!

Meanwhile during the past week Char had worked on her sea plane as well. She brought her finished project to the kitchen table and set it next to mine. It was small, it was simple, it was neat, and it was *orange*. "Cute", I thought, "but definitely not a contender."

The next Saturday, we walked to the store with our finished creations in hand. I beamed with pride at my achievement and couldn't wait to show it off.

The store was buzzing with excitement. In the middle of the room were two long tables covered with dark blue tablecloths made of felt. Three huge trophies made of wood, marble, and gold, rested on top. They were flanked by a few entries already placed on the tables. More kids, all carrying models, filed into the store.

Char and I made our way through the crowd and handed our models and entry cards to the man in charge. I felt like a mother handing her newborn baby to a stranger. I couldn't take my eyes off it until I saw it placed safely on the table. Char's plane was next to mine. We both waited for the judging to begin.

I'm not sure who the judge was or what made him the authority on model building. Maybe he was a "Master Model Builder" like the banner read out front, or maybe he was Mr. Revell! Whoever he was, he held the hopes and dreams of the fifty or so kids present in his hands.

Anticipation mounted as the final entries were placed on the tables. The store became quiet as a mortuary. All eyes were on the judge as he went to work.

He slowly circled the tables studying each entry like a chess player. He even put his glasses on when he leaned down to get a closer look at the subjects. I was sure he was making mental notes. "Great," I thought, "he'll catch all the details of my bi-plane including the fully adjustable stabilizers free from glue drips. He'll even see how neat the paint is on the helmets of the pilot and co-pilot!"

The more time he spent scrutinizing the entries the better for me. After a few more nerve-racking minutes, he was ready to make his decision. The moment of truth was finally at hand.

He grabbed one of the trophies and walked to the far side of the table. He placed the trophy on the table and, like a Grand Master in a game of chess, slid it across the felt. It stopped adjacent to a candy apple red 1940 Ford Coupe.

Repeating that move with another gold statue he placed the second trophy next to a fully camouflaged military helicopter.

With one trophy remaining he carefully considered his options. He walked around the table again and placed the final trophy on the felt. He was moving in super slow motion as he slid it across the felt for the last time. It came to rest next to *my* bi-plane. At that instant my life changed. I couldn't think straight. I was about to explode with excitement!

He then stepped back from the table, looked over his three selections, and like a chess player about to proclaim "check mate," he grinned as if confirming the brilliance of his choices.

Immediately my eyes cut a path through the crowd as I envisioned myself walking to the front to claim my prize. All the tedious planning, patience, and determination — not to mention skill — was about to be rewarded. The biggest trophy I'd ever seen was sitting next to my bi-plane waiting for me to claim it.

But wait....something was wrong. The judge returned to the table as if having second thoughts. In chess, when you take your hand off a piece you just moved, the move was over, you couldn't change your mind. But this obviously *wasn't* a game of chess. He walked around the entries again studying them even harder. What could he possibly be doing? I held my breath, my head spinning. And then without the slightest bit of remorse he took *my* trophy and slid it next to the orange sea plane!

I *gasped* at the sight. Like a boxer being hit by a left hook coming out of nowhere, I was stunned and dazed. The judge turned to the crowd and said, "Well, these are the winners. Let's give the kids a nice hand, they ALL did a great job."

The contest was over and so was my life. As the crowd began to disperse, I stood frozen in time. I was unable to comprehend what had just happened. The applause was replaced by the sound of kids slapping the winners on the back. I approached the table to collect my entry and gazed at the sea plane and the trophy next to it. Char had done a pretty good

job. Except for the color the plane was actually
flawless.

We made our way home without much
conversation. Char carried her orange sea plane in
one hand and the trophy in the other. I couldn't make
sense of it. The number of parts, the paint, the decals,
the time, it just didn't add up. I felt disappointed and
confused. And Char seemed to understand.

But these feelings didn't last forever. The hurt
associated with not winning the contest lessened over
time and before long Char and I were back to doing
what we did best, just hanging out.

Years later the memory of the contest began to
resurface and so did a possible explanation. Somehow
the judge who gave the award to Char had seen
something in her creation that mine lacked. In its
simplicity a certain honesty emerged from the orange
sea plane. And maybe he could tell that whoever built
it had built it from their heart. He was right. I had been
so wrapped up in what I was doing that I failed to notice
the good job Char was doing.

There were four winners that day: the builder of the 1940 Ford Coupe, the camouflaged helicopter, and my sister Char, with her little orange sea plane. And even though my entry didn't win, I learned something important that day.

It's not always what you accomplish in life that counts, but rather how you go about it. Doing something with honesty and a good heart is more important than showing off. Char had done her best, for all the right reasons, and no one deserved to win more than she did. Having learned that, I was a winner too.

HIGH FLYER

"You must do the thing you think you cannot do."
Eleanor Roosevelt

Freeways were born in California in the early fifties. As a by-product of their birth, entire neighborhoods were systematically torn down, house by house, block by block, all in the name of something called "eminent domain." I thought that meant the freeways were more important than the families living in their proposed paths. Although the house we rented (it was actually the front unit of a duplex) was spared, the house next door was erased from the landscape as well as all the houses on both sides of the street behind us.

After the demolition crew came and leveled the neighbor's house all that remained was a trench as wide as a two lane highway and a good five feet deep. The trench would eventually be paved for the freeway off-ramp. Like a hot dog waiting for mustard the trench lay waiting for concrete to be poured over it. It was during this brief window of opportunity that I almost lost my life.

At the time of the construction my sister Char owned a really cool bike. It was cool for a number of reasons. First, it was built like a Chrysler Imperial. Forged of heavy-duty steel it easily outweighed any kid who would climb aboard it.

Second, it had balloon tires, the first bike of its kind in the family. Up until then all the bikes we rode had solid rubber tires. These were impervious to going flat but rolled as slow as molasses. Balloon tires on the other hand made the bike faster than a new pair of P.F. Flyers!

Finally, it had coaster brakes which meant the rider could turn that blinding speed into a skid mark as long as a car. And because it was built like a Sherman Tank it could take some serious abuse. This bike in the right hands could take a kid to new heights. And I was at the age to provide those hands. The possibilities were endless and exciting.

One day my sister Char mentioned something astonishing. She said she'd ridden this bike and actually jumped over the new trench, sailing through the air and landing safely without incident a good distance from the launch point.

Mesmerized by the details of her accomplishment I listened to how she managed to pull it off. I could tell from the tone of her voice that she wasn't making any of this up. Why would she? She had accomplished something I hadn't, something bold and daring, and I knew I needed to do the same.

Up until now the only time I'd seen anything like what she had described was on TV involving a motorcycle. Imagine the feeling she must have felt flying through the air sailing over the trench far below! Knowing the bike was capable of such a stunt the only question that remained was this, "Did I have the guts to try such a maneuver? If Char, my younger sister by a year had done it, I could do the same, couldn't I?" I looked at the yellow iron horse with a new set of eyes, determined to take the challenge myself.

The task at hand was a big one. To actually fly over the trench, several critical elements needed to be present. First, I would need an enormous amount of speed. The laws of physics told me that the heavier an object the more force was required to move it. The bike weighed a ton, so to get it to sail through the air meant I would need speed approaching terminal velocity. I knew the balloon tires would now be worth their weight in gold.

Next, perfect timing would be essential. I would have to wait until the absolute last second possible, just before the bike was about to go over the edge, to pull up on the handlebars in order to direct the bike skyward. Once in the air I would need to keep the bike balanced to insure a perfect landing.

If I could put all these elements together, I thought I too would know what Char felt and quite possibly know the same feeling the Wright brothers must have felt at Kittyhawk. The only thing to fear now was fear itself.

I stood at the edge of the trench looking down, carefully selecting the point to jump from. I saw where I would land if everything went according to plan. This would be across the trench about twenty feet from the take-off point. It was a long way to the bottom of the trench. If I was an only child I probably would have scratched the whole idea. But the fact that my *younger* sister had already accomplished this prodded me onward. I had no choice but to continue.

I selected a starting point about a hundred yards down the street. Speed was my primary concern. Like a pilot in the cockpit of a DC-3 before takeoff I put the iron beast through a series of checks. The seat was securely attached, handlebars straight, chain taut (although the chain guard was gone), tire pressure good, and except for one missing handlebar grip, the vehicle was ready.

Before mounting the bike I rolled up my right pant leg to avoid getting caught in the chain and I climbed aboard. A voice inside was screaming, telling me to abandon the whole idea. I was scared but not afraid. I prepared for launch.

As I began to pedal I focused on the spot I was going to jettison from. I pedaled harder and harder. My heart pounded as the bike and I raced toward my destiny. Within seconds I was going so fast that if the bike had wings, it could have flown!

My eyes were locked on the targeted position which was rapidly approaching. Was I going fast enough? Could I control the pitch of the bike once I became airborne? And most importantly would I be able to land the bike safely like Char did? All these questions collided in my brain without a single answer. Adrenaline replaced reason!

And just as I approached the point of no return, traveling at what seemed like a hundred miles an hour, a fraction of a second before the front wheel was about to go over the cliff, an answer came screaming from deep within my soul, "NOOOOO!"

Instinctively I slammed on the brakes in a futile attempt to abort the mission. But it was too late. All I could do was hold on as the speed I worked so hard to produce, dissipated. Human flesh and forged metal plummeted in a twisted free fall to the bottom of the trench.

The taste of dirt was a good indication that I was still alive. Then a burning sensation over my right eye was followed by darkness. I had sight in my left eye only. Blood warmed my cheek as it flowed from above my eye. I pushed the bike off my battered body, crawled to my knees, and attempted to get my bearings. The bike was fine, I wasn't. The missing handlebar grip now revealed its true purpose. The bare end of the steel handlebar had gouged my head just above my right eye. At least I was still alive.

Instinctively I covered the gash with a dirty hand. Dazed, I made my way to the back door of my house and because it was locked, I began kicking it. "I fell off the bike," I said as my mom opened the door. "Oh my God," she screamed, as she swooped me into her arms and carried me to the kitchen sink. She held my head under cold running water to get a better look at the cut. "Stitches," was her diagnosis.

About an hour later I returned from the hospital with four stitches over my eye and a huge bandage that made the injury look worse than it actually was. The doctor said that if the cut was a hairline lower, I'd have lost an eye.

Defeated, I had to tell Char that I was unable to pull off the same stunt she had accomplished a few days earlier. She listened sympathetically as I explained the details of my failed attempt. "Where exactly did you try and make the jump from?" she asked. When I explained that it was over the deepest part of the trench she shook her head. "That's probably why it didn't work," she pointed out. "I jumped about 50 yards from where you tried, at a point where the trench was about five inches deep, NOT five feet!

With this revelation the pain over my right eye hurt even more. It was the one piece of information that could have changed everything. Instead I had four stitches, sore ribs, a bruised shoulder, and had almost lost an eye. All because I was trying to do something I thought Char had done.

The attempted jump and resulting crash taught me some things. First, don't take chances before knowing all the risks involved. Secondly, whenever you try something that could result in grave danger, take a few safety precautions. Third, don't let someone else — even if it is your sister — lead you to risk your life. Life's too short for stupid stuff like that.

SAFE AT HOME

My first real contact with organized baseball came when I was about eight years old. George the Baker, who drove the Helm's truck that delivered bread to our neighborhood, recruited me to be the bat boy for a Pony League team called the Braves. The players wore real uniforms, wore real steel cleats, and played on a baseball diamond with fences that seemed like they were a mile away.

The infield was dragged and watered before the chalk lines were laid. The scoreboard in left field had real working lights that not only called out the score, but also showed the count and number of outs.

The umpires continued the look of professionalism by wearing the traditional black slacks, black turtleneck sweater and black suit jacket. They also had nicknames like "One Eye" and "Bones". Everything about this level of baseball was exciting. This was the "Big Time."

As the official bat boy of the Braves I was issued a uniform. It was sized for a teenager and it was huge. The pants went all the way to the top of my high topped sneakers and were held in place by a black belt which was about twelve inches too long. The shirt sleeves came down to the middle of my forearms. The oversized cap came to rest on my somewhat adult-sized ears. But none of these size flaws mattered to me except maybe the size of my ears. When I put the uniform on I was a Brave. And I took my new assignment very seriously.

The first game of the season was at 5 p.m. at the Pony League field in Culver City. I rode with George the Baker, who managed the team, and we arrived about a half hour before game time. He briefed me on the duties of a bat boy and I proceeded to go to work. I removed the bats from the equipment bag and hung them in the bat rack just outside the dugout. I lined up the batter's helmets at the base of the bats and rolled the warm-up balls from the bottom of the equipment bag. With everything in place I was ready for the game to begin.

The umpire yelled, "Play ball!" as I took my place halfway down the dugout steps eagerly waiting to go to work. My first opportunity was about to unfold.

The lead off batter struck out and therefore returned his bat to the rack unassisted. The next batter drew a walk and as he trotted to first, he threw his bat toward the dugout. I climbed the stairs, picked up the piece of wood, and like a dog retrieving the Sunday paper, I faithfully returned it to the bat rack.

One out, man on first, and the next batter steps into the box. The pitcher looks in for the signal, shakes off the first one and sets. Not much of a lead at first, he winds and throws. The ball is driven up the alley in left center and rolls to the fence. This was going for extra bases. With runners charging around the bases the center fielder races to get the ball. The relay man, I think he was the short stop, gets into position as the throw is about to come in from the outfield.

Meanwhile I'm gazing at the bat which is lying across home plate, extending into the batter's box. Everything around me ceased to exist except that bat. What was I suppose to do now?

Options raced through my head at the speed of light. If the runner came sliding into home and landed on the bat, it would definitely be my fault. My first day on the job would most likely be my last. On the other hand if I retrieve the bat before the arrival of the runner, I'd be clearing the way so the bat wouldn't interfere with the play. Was that my *real* job? Leave it there? Run and grab it? I had but a second to make my decision. I opted to go for the bat.

Focusing on the bat I made my move. As the lead runner was tearing around third at full throttle, I climbed the steps of the dugout and headed full speed for the bat. The catcher, who was positioning himself to receive the throw, was not only blocking the plate but was straddling the bat. Bones, the umpire, had come around in front of the catcher positioning himself to make the call. The runner was bearing down upon the plate, getting ready to go into his slide, just as I entered the scene. The catcher, the runner, the ball, the bat and I, all converged on home plate at the same time. The crash was cataclysmic. When the dust finally settled, I was laying on my back looking up into barely recognizable faces, still clutching the bat.

It was Bones who spoke first. "Are you O.K. son?" I think he said while attempting to help me up. Although I felt like I'd been run over by a herd of buffalo I nodded that I was all right. George the Baker was there too and, after helping me to my feet, guided me to the dugout.

As I passed the bat rack I faithfully placed the bat I was still holding back where it belonged. I walked down the steps to the dugout but instead of assuming my regular position halfway down, I went all the way to the bench. I sat there for a few minutes just trying to get my bearings. This job was definitely going to be more dangerous than I thought!

As I sat trying to remember what day it was, the other team's manager was arguing that the runner should have been called out because I had interfered with the play. I could hear him shouting that "the batboy had no right to impede the progress of play." After going nose to nose with Bones and getting nowhere, he advised the ump that he was playing the game under protest. He wanted the run taken away and that was that. My first game as bat boy and they're filing protests because of me!

George the Baker came down into the dugout and asked me how I was doing. I smiled to let him know I was still prepared to do my duties when he said, "Next time wait until the play is over before you get the bat." Nothing ever sounded so logical. I nodded so he knew I understood.

After the game when I walked in the house my mom took one look at me and said, "How'd you get so dirty just being a bat boy?" I just didn't feel like going into it. I peeled off the uniform, slipped into the warm bath water and replayed the entire event over and over in my head. I'd nearly been killed on the job and I felt like a complete jerk, but now I was safe at home.

After that incident I took a different approach to my duties as a bat boy. I settled into a routine of getting the bat *after* the play was over no matter where the batter had left it. It seemed to work out good for everyone and was definitely safer for me. I finished the season virtually unscathed. I got to know old Bones pretty well too and he'd always say something encouraging to me whenever I retrieved a bat.

When the season with the Braves was over, I graduated from bat boy to being a player in Little League. I soon forgot about the blunder I made that night that nearly cost us the game and almost cost me my life. And I learned some things about the game of baseball and about life as well.

Everyone on a team needs to do their part. No matter how big or small their job is each member needs to do their best. In baseball, as in life, it's often the small things that can make the difference between winning and losing. The details should never be overlooked. And finally, and most importantly, I learned that timing is everything.

WHEELS OF FORTUNE

Sometimes even I can't believe my luck. It all started on a Saturday afternoon when I was ten years old. I had walked to the barber shop to get a flat top — a haircut that made anyone who got one look like a Marine. While the barber buzzed away he casually mentioned that he had a bicycle for sale. "Oh," I said. "What kind of bicycle?" The barber then showed why he was better at cutting hair than describing the details of a bicycle. He searched for a descriptive word or phrase that would make the bike appealing to me, but not knowing even the most basic terms used to describe a bike's features, he settled on a generic nondescript phrase, "Well it's just about your size."

This told me nothing. What I needed to know were the particulars. What kind of handlebars did it have, a goose neck with butterflies? What kind of seat, banana or regular? Street tires or knobbies? Coaster brakes, hand brakes, or both? These were the features that determined whether a bike was cool or not.

"Why don't you come back around 3 o'clock and I'll have it here for you to look at," he said as he finished leveling the top of my head. I jumped down from the huge red leather chair, glanced in one of the mirrors that adorned every wall to check out his handiwork, and handed him two shiny quarters. I agreed to come back in the afternoon.

I ran home to discuss this with mom. Although dad made the money there was no doubt that mom managed it. If the deal was to go through I'd need mom's support.

I opened the back door which led to the kitchen. "Your haircut looks great," she said. "Do you like it mom?" I replied. "Hey mom, the barber is selling a bike, do you think we could go look at it later this afternoon?" I injected the subject into the conversation right away. The expression on my mom's face usually indicated whether it was a good time to ask for something or not. She seemed pretty receptive at the moment so I continued. "The barber said he'd have it at the shop around three this afternoon. What do you say we take a look?" "How much is he asking for it?" she replied. "I think he mentioned $20."

She walked into her bedroom and I could hear the brass handles click against the maple dresser as she pulled open the drawer. I could see her thumbing through a stack of envelopes she used to put money in for the rent, groceries, telephone, etc. She removed one of the envelopes and closed the drawer. She agreed to go with me later in the day.

My mom didn't drive so we walked to the barber shop which was about a mile from our house. I kept thinking about the bike and hoping it would be cool. We entered the shop and found the barber reading a newspaper sitting in the same big red chair I'd been in just hours earlier. "Hey kiddo, I see you came back. Let me show you the bike."

Surrounded by mirrors and the smell of talcum powder, we waited as he disappeared through a hallway which led to the back room. Moments later he emerged with the bike.

It was a Schwinn Sting Ray, candy apple red, with a two inch goose neck, butterfly handle bars, chrome fenders and knobby tires. A banana seat and coaster brakes completed the package. Except for a few small scratches on the paint and some wear on the tires, it was definitely cool.

I took it outside for a test ride. Besides looking good, the Sting Ray handled great. It felt like it was made just for me!

Mom sensed that I wanted this bike and she smiled with approval. She confirmed the price with the barber, paid for it with money she took out of the envelope from her dresser, and just like that we were on our way home. The deal was done.

Walking along side my mom I pushed the bike to the corner. After we crossed the boulevard I jumped on the bike and rode. Riding a bike does something to a kid. It creates a feeling of freedom. As I raced down the street with the wind blowing in my face, I embraced this new found freedom and the feeling of power that came with it.

For the next two weeks I rode my bike everywhere, riding further from home than I'd ever been before. And I would have continued my ventures except for one small mishap — the bike got a flat tire. Normally this wouldn't have been that big of a deal but this time it led to something quite unusual.

My dad was good at a lot of things. He was a star runner in high school, setting the state record in the mile. He spent a lot of time with us kids taking us to the park and on rides to Frosty Freeze. He was also a good provider. But my dad, by his own admission, was not mechanically inclined. He never even pretended to be. In fact, the only tools he owned were a pair of pliers, one screw driver and a ball-peen hammer. To this day I have no idea why this kind of hammer was even invented. With a ball-peen hammer you can't even remove a nail because there isn't a claw at either end!

He kept this primitive assortment of tools in a drawer in the kitchen appropriately known as the "junk drawer." Consequently, any project requiring the use of a tool beyond what could be found in the "junk drawer" was going to require an inordinate amount of time and ingenuity. Fixing a flat tire was well beyond the limits of his mechanical ability, so the task took on enormous proportions. The only real option was to have the flat fixed by a professional. The following Saturday we took the bike to Wheel World, the biggest bike shop in the county, and checked it into their equally impressive repair shop.

I didn't realize how much I'd miss my bike until I had to walk to school for an entire week. Having a flat was disrupting my life, but the following Saturday dad and I drove to the bike shop to retrieve my rehabilitated bike. We entered the huge store walking past rows and rows of new bikes, there must have been over a hundred, to the rear of the store where the repair counter was located.

Huddled next to the counter was a sad looking lot of definitely used and obviously broken bikes. There were bikes with bent wheels, broken chains, missing seats and flat tires. Each bike in this area had a red repair tag, like the wrist bands patients wear in the hospital, dangling from the handle bars. These bikes all looked pretty sick to me.

As my dad reached in his wallet for the claim check, I scanned the cluster of bikes expecting to see mine. Not there. "That's funny," I thought. "It must still be in the back probably getting the finishing touches to the repair." The man who was with my dad took the claim check and disappeared into the shop. We waited, for what seemed like forever, for my bike to come rolling out from the back. Finally the man returned...empty handed.

He moved to the group of bikes I had just surveyed. "What color bike are we looking for?" he asked nervously. As I began to describe my bike, he glanced at the claim check trying to match up the numbers with a bike. No luck. He looked somewhat frantic now as he was beginning to realize what I already knew. He couldn't match the numbers on the claim check with a bike because something was obviously missing...my bike! His expression now turned to panic.

He checked again in the workshop and then walked to the front of the store where the manager sat. They huddled in quiet conversation. Shoulders shrugged, heads shook, arms flailed and before they reached agreement, my dad and I both realized what was coming. It was no surprise when the manager announced, "I'm afraid the bike isn't here."

"What did you say?" replied my dad. "What exactly do you mean it isn't here?" my dad said firmly.

"Well, I think we may have accidentally sold your son's bike," the manager said nervously. Silence followed.

What my dad lacked in mechanical ability he more than made up for in tenacity. Like a chess player pondering his next move he mentally outlined a strategy. Dad was first to break the silence. "If you don't have my son's bike back in one week, I'll bring my attorney down here to straighten this thing out," he said. Dad was going for "checkmate." To be honest I don't think my dad knew how to play chess, and he definitely didn't know an attorney. But he'd taken a gutsy position and dug in. The next move was up to the owner of the bike shop.

We left the store just as we had entered — empty handed. I knew dad had a plan but I wasn't sure how it would unfold. Later that night I found out.

Dad phoned my mom's brother-in-law, Uncle Bob, and invited him and his family to dinner the following Saturday. "Would you wear a suit when you come next weekend?" I heard him ask. "And bring a briefcase! I'll explain when you get here." The plan was simple yet brilliant. Using Uncle Bob as a shill, he would call their bluff.

Uncle Bob arrived wearing a three piece suit, carrying a black leather briefcase, and looking like F. Lee Bailey, the famous criminal attorney. Dad briefed him on the details and then the three of us returned to Wheel World — the scene of the crime. We marched in and flanked the counter waiting for the perpetrators to appear. The manager and salesman emerged from the rear of the store.

With no introductions offered or needed my dad spoke. "Well do you have the bike?" The manager nervously glanced at my Uncle Bob and his briefcase. Without the slightest hesitation, probably because he really had no choice, the manager answered. "No, I wasn't able to find your son's bike…but I'd like to offer a solution." They took the bait. "What if your son picks out a *new* bike instead?" The words cascaded from Heaven.

I looked at my dad who looked at Uncle Bob who was looking at me. "What do you say about that Jimmy, would that be O.K. with you?" said my dad in a business like voice. I could hardly contain myself. "Sounds terrific," I said.

I slowly walked aisle after aisle of new bikes, feeling like I'd just won the Irish Sweep Stakes, and picked out a brand new bike — my first new set of wheels.

Uncle Bob never said a word during the entire ordeal. Once in the car he broke his silence. "I'm just glad they didn't ask for my business card," he said as he loosened his tie and began to chuckle. Minutes later we were home and as the adults talked about the ordeal, I was riding my new bike.

In a matter of weeks I went from riding a used bike I'd bought at a barber shop to being the proud owner of a brand new bike. And I realized that my dad's lack of mechanical ability wasn't nearly as important as his ability to resolve a problem.

"Take the Pitch"

In life the difference between winning and losing can often be determined by one single identifiable event. In baseball that one event can be a play, a hit, or a pitch. Although the event may represent but a minuscule portion of the whole, its significance can become far greater and its impact enormous. The success or failure of an entire season can sometimes hinge on one such event. I was ten years old when I committed the biggest blunder of my young baseball career and discovered this first hand.

It was my second year playing organized ball. I was on the Indians and because it was my first year playing with the ten and eleven year olds, I was relegated to playing second string second base. Playing second string didn't bother me though because this was an awesome team. Our pin stripped uniforms looked cool and we were named after a real big league team.

But the exciting thing about this team were the players. We had some great hitters! Five of our starters each hit at least five home runs. This was more home runs by far than any other team in the league. Mickey DeFay, Jack Callahan, Alex Schumacher and Bruce Howell were teammates with names that sounded like they belonged in the Big Leagues. Being on this team, even sitting on the bench, was a thrill.

Mr. Schumacher, Alex's dad, was our manager. He was the kind of person who rarely got excited about anything. During every game he'd position himself at the top of the stairs leading to the dugout and eat sunflower seeds the entire game. He'd occasionally shout out encouragement to us players by clapping his hands and yelling, "Come now babe," as he popped another handful of seeds in his mouth.

Although I spent the majority of the season sitting on the bench watching my teammates beat every other team in the league, I occasionally entered the game as a pinch hitter. My stature, not my hitting ability, was the reason I was selected for this role.

Being the shortest kid on the team meant a small strike zone and this improved my chances of drawing a walk. And most of the time I did. I got pretty good at reaching first in this fashion.

In a game against the Orioles it was the bottom of the last inning and we were down by one run. With two outs and the bases loaded, Mr. Schumacher looked to the bench for a suitable pinch hitter. He gave me the nod. I sprang to my feet, climbed the stairs out of the dugout and proceeded to the bat rack. I selected the lightest bat in the arsenal, grabbed a batting helmet, and stood in the on-deck circle taking a few practice swings. A few good swings and I was loose. I walked to the batter's box with the confidence of a bull fighter, pulled up on my pants, and stepped up to the plate. The game was on the line and I was ready.

I peered out to the mound and waited to see what kind of stuff the pitcher had. The wind-up and the pitch: ball one. I stepped out of the box and glanced down to third. Mr. Schumacher went through a series of fake signs. The real signs were rehearsed prior to every game. I resumed my place at the plate: ball two.

The tension was mounting. The pitcher was beginning to struggle.

The next pitch was critical. Another ball and he'd be in a hole and I'd be one step closer to reaching first and bringing in the winning run. Another check with Mr. Schumacher — still nothing going on — and I'm back in the batter's box. The next pitch was a fast ball that sailed a foot over my head. The count was exactly what I wanted. Three balls no strikes.

The pitcher was up to his ears in alligators. Another pitch like that, I'd go to first, a run would score, and I'd be the hero.

Mr. Schumacher motioned to the umpire for time. Removing his mask, raising his hands into the air, the ump yelled at the top of his lungs, "Time out!" Mr. Schumacher motioned for me to come to him. We met half way down the line. Kneeling on one knee Mr. Schumacher put one hand on my shoulder and his other hand over his mouth. "Whatever you do," he whispered, *"take the pitch."*

Like God himself enunciating one of the Ten Commandments to Moses the words were perfectly clear. Only I wasn't Moses and he wasn't God. He gave me a pat on the butt and walked back to the coach's box, spitting a few seeds along the way.

I turned and walked back to the batter's box letting his instructions settle in my brain. I understood the magnitude of the moment, everyone did. It was all up to me. The crowd fell silent. The chatter usually provided by the infielders before each pitch was muted. I pulled up on my pants again and prepared to take my place in history.

There was only one minor problem. In my entire life I'd never heard the phrase "take the pitch" before. The words echoed in my head like a bell in a church tower. I struggled to make sense of them.

As I stepped between the lines of the batter's box I had no idea what I was supposed to do. Was I supposed to swing? How does someone "take a pitch"? Take it where? If he didn't want me to swing, he'd have said, "Don't swing." But was that correct? I could find no certain logic in the words just spoken. The words "take the pitch" could have been Arabic, for they meant absolutely nothing to me.

Then I thought "Mr. Schumacher has something up his sleeve." Like every great commander in the heat of battle, Mr. Schumacher was ordering something to surprise the enemy. When everyone expected me to walk, maybe Mr. Schumacher was giving me the order to "take the pitch" and blast it! Time was running out. The pitcher had started his wind-up. The moment had arrived. I made a decision.

As the ball left the pitcher's hand I began my swing. I immediately knew the pitch was going to be tough to hit because it was coming high and a little off the plate. But I was committed. I threw the bat out over the plate at the precise moment the ball was crossing it. Crack! The sweetest sound in the world pierced the air. The ball was on its way. I had "taken the pitch" as instructed and ripped it.

But instead of going out where it should have gone, the ball went up, almost straight up. The pitcher waved everyone else off, positioned himself comfortably under it, and caught it. Just like that the game was over.

In the year I'd played for Mr. Schumacher I had never seen him raise his voice, get mad, or even get excited. But all that changed thanks to me. Mr. Schumacher grabbed his cap, threw it into the ground and with hundreds of sunflower seeds shooting from his mouth, yelled my name at the top of his lungs. Kneeling down on one knee next to me — with the veins in his neck bulging like worms — he placed both his hands on my shoulders. He probably wanted to put them around my neck!

After pausing to catch his breath he spoke in the same clear manner as before. "When I say 'take the pitch' I mean *don't* swing, *don't* hit the ball, let the ball pass you by, whatever you do, do NOTHING!"

Any of these explanations would have made sense to me minutes earlier. And now "take the pitch" also made sense. But it was too late. The damage had been done and one single event had turned an entire game around. Not only was the game over, but so was my life.

The walk to the car with my dad after the game took forever. He gave me one of his "Jimmy, you play like a rubber boot" lectures. Obviously a rubber boot can't play ball at all so this was his way of saying I'd messed up big time. He wasn't going to get an argument from me on this one.

As I lay in bed that night I replayed the game in my head. I couldn't believe I'd made the mistake of trying to hit that ball. Even though I'd tried my best we still lost. Sometimes life is like that. But you can't let the fear of losing stop you from trying. Losing is part of life too.

The important thing is to learn something from every mistake you make. Turn a negative into a positive. And when all the dust settles, you'll have more wins than loses and have become a better person along the way.

THE TAXICAB KID

When I was a kid I had big ears, I mean *really* big ears. Vin Scully, the play by play announcer for the Dodgers, who also owned an oversized pair of ears when he was a kid, said he looked like a "taxicab with its doors open." That pretty much described me too.

I didn't need reminding that I had big ears, but other people thought I did. When I was about seven or so, standing next to my mom while she talked to a neighbor, I distinctly heard Mrs. Chudler say, "Little pictures have big ears." These words cut like a knife when they landed on my over-sized protrusions. That single phrase confirmed for me that my ears were going to bring me a lot of grief in the years to come.

I was in the 5th grade when my real problems began. Having big ears and a name like Jimmy spelled disaster. I had a bad feeling about this combination from the beginning. For some unknown reason, "Jimmy" quickly turned into "Jimbo," a name I hated the first time I heard it. For God's sake "Jimmy" was already a nickname for "Jim" which was a nickname for "James," so how many more nicknames does one person need? Maybe it was just me and the fact that I was lugging around these prominent ears that made me a little oversensitive. But I knew something for sure. "Jimbo" without question would evolve into "Jumbo" and for someone with big ears that would be the kiss of death. Patty Imonte was the first one to make the inevitable connection.

Sister Gertrudis, the nun assigned to the 5th grade class at St. Gerard Majella School, had left the classroom to go to the office. As usual she instructed the class to remain seated and silent until she returned. During her absence she left Patty in charge. Patty, a fellow classmate, took this appointment way too seriously.

She perched herself in Sister Gertrudis' chair clutching a piece of chalk like an assassin holding a gun, fully prepared to inscribe on the blackboard the names of anyone in violation of the gag order. Within minutes the usual names went up on the board; David W., Tommy V., and Kenny H. Even though this was only the 5th grade these names had already become infamous.

I was Patty's next victim. She quickly added "Jimmy M." to the list after she'd seen me whispering to Johnny Zimmerman. She then tossed me one of her patented smirks as if to say, "Sorry Jimmy, but you deserve it!" There I sat, surrounded by thirty-five or so classmates, staring at my name and considering my fate. Meanwhile Patty resumed her post in the guard tower.

And then, completely unprovoked, as if struck by a bolt of creativity that had been forming for a million years, Patty went back to the board. With one simple stroke of an eraser she removed "Jimmy" and replaced it with "Jimbo."

I took the bullet directly in the heart. Blood rushed to my head igniting my ears. I was aware of nothing beside the name on the board and my burning ears.

As my breathing shortened and my chest pounded I knew deep within my soul what was coming next. With the barrel of the gun still smoking, Patty reloaded and fired one more round. She returned to the board and replaced "Jimbo" with the most loathsome word in the English language. When she finished writing and moved aside, my name had become "Jumbo M." The class erupted in laughter as I gasped. This shot was fatal.

There it was emblazoned in front of the world, a combination of letters that spelled total and complete humiliation for me, and it hung like a name on a Broadway marquee. The name had now entered the collective consciousness of the entire class and as a result, my fate was sealed. Any hope of escaping this moniker was dashed forever with one stroke of Patty's chalk. I was sure my life was over at that point.

It seemed like hours before the nun returned and erased the names. When the bell rang to end the school day I dejectedly made my way home. My self-esteem had been annihilated. The one thing I knew for certain was that I despised the ears I was saddled with. It was the worst day of my life.

As I lay in bed that night, reliving the day's events, I knew I had to do something to "fix" my ears if I was going to make it through life. I had once heard of a kid with big ears getting them "pinned." This sounded like a painful procedure but given my situation, pain was the least of my worries. I would endure anything to alleviate the problem. But in my family money was always tight and elective surgery wasn't an option. If I was going to change my situation I knew I'd have to take a non-surgical approach, and I'd have to do it myself.

I thought about the possibilities every waking moment for a week before a plan unfolded. My mom frequently reminded us kids that we needed to get plenty of sleep. According to her, "kids grew when they slept." I reasoned that if my body was growing while I slept, my ears were growing as well. If I slept on my side, my pillow would press my ear against my head for eight hours. By alternating sides each night, I could guide my ears into place as they grew. The process might be a little slow, but it would cost nothing to try and, if it worked, would pay the ultimate dividend.

I began that night. And every night thereafter I religiously followed my plan. I told no one of this ritual. If my reasoning was correct my ears were growing into a more normal position. It would just be a matter of time before my problem would be fixed.

During the day I was an ordinary school kid with big ears. At night I was on a mission using a technique I had developed myself. It was a long-shot but I had no other options. I had nothing to lose and everything to gain.

After several months of this routine there was a breakthrough. I began to notice something quite unusual. Fewer and fewer classmates were making comments about my ears. Was this process actually working? Most of the time my fellow classmates were simply calling me "Jimmy" and nothing else. No one but me noticed this social phenomenon. Was the nightly therapy I developed the reason for this change, or was my head growing to match my ears? The reason was unimportant to me only the results mattered. My ears were evolving, slowly but certainly, to a near normal position on my head. And a giant load was being lifted from my shoulders. I was ecstatic.

And then, for the first time in my life, the seeds of self-confidence began to germinate. During the remainder of the school year I actually began to focus on people and events *around* me instead of worrying about how my ears made me look. The feeling was one of complete relief.

During the same year I was elected class president. The following year I was elected class representative on the student council. From that time forward I was able to leave the problems associated with my ears behind me.

While some people might say that having big ears and being forced to live with them is the kind of thing that builds character, I disagree. My big ears brought me a lot of grief, ridicule, and self-doubt. But in the end I realized that people look the way they do for a million different reasons. Things like heredity, genes, and a bunch of other factors go into making up the way we look. And as long as people look different kids will make fun of them. Sadly, no one has any control over these things.

I don't really know for certain how my ears found their way to a near normal position on my head; sometimes I think it might have been a miracle! But I do know one thing — whatever the reason — the "Taxicab Kid" was able to close the doors.

PRESSURE POINTS

My dad spent a few years in prison, not behind bars as a prisoner, but on the other side as a guard. We lived in San Pedro at the time on a street named Sea Cliff Circle. Every so often my dad and I would take the ferry over to the place he worked, Terminal Island Correctional Facility, and we'd both get our hair cut. Imagine trying to relax in a barber chair while felons convicted of murder, extortion, and rape, stood behind you holding straight razors and other tools of the trade. I could see the headline, "Eight Year Old Boy Used as Human Shield in Daring Prison Break, film at 11!" Fortunately, I was too young to fully comprehend the risks involved or to question dad's wisdom in choosing to have our hair cut in this environment.

A free haircut by a felon was only one benefit of having a dad that worked in a prison. In addition, I was able to learn a unique skill that would set me apart from every other kid in school. A skill only my dad could teach me.

Working as a prison guard required my dad to be adept in the martial arts: karate and judo primarily. Although he never displayed any of these skills at home, I felt reasonably certain he used them every time he went to work. Just knowing dad possessed these skills gave me an incredible feeling of security while growing up. I would have felt sorry for anyone who might cross my dad the wrong way. He'd dissect them with one quick karate chop to the throat, if he wanted to. I felt that no harm could ever come to our family while dad was around. And I patiently waited for the day when he'd teach me these time honored skills.

I was in the seventh grade when playing kickball and four-square gave way to a more physical activity during recess. The new recess play resembled the ancient art of wrestling and it was conducted exclusively by the boys. It was a harmless exercise that also provided an outlet for the male hormone testosterone developing in each of us.

Being the second shortest kid in the class, I quickly realized that my lack of size and weight was a distinct disadvantage when wrestling. To enhance my ability to compete with bigger boys, I turned to my dad for help. Now was the time to add to my arsenal the skills only he could teach me. I made the official request. I wanted to learn the martial arts, the moves he'd utilized while working as a prison guard. I wanted to learn karate, judo, or maybe a combination of both.

My dad considered the request for weeks before giving me an answer. After all, you don't reveal techniques that are capable of killing another human being without a little discretion and thought. "Son, we need to talk," dad began. "There are a lot of things I could teach you about self-defense but it all boils down to one thing." He was going to cut to the chase I thought. His years of self-discipline and rigid training in this area were going to be given to me in a Readers Digest condensed version. What more could I ask for?

Armed with the secret information he was about to reveal, my body would be transformed into a fortress, my mind raised to a higher level. On the wrestling mat the next day I would become "the ultimate weapon." Like a dog waiting for a bone I waited for dad to tell me the *one thing* that would make all this possible, one-on-one, man-to-man.

The time had come. My training was about to begin. The Master was going to reveal the *one thing.* Looking me directly in the eye, dad uttered two words that struck me as profound. *"Pressure points,"* he said. Neither of us spoke as I let the sacred words settle in my brain. Pressure points? That was it? Two words? Was he kidding? What the heck was he talking about anyway?

"Let me explain it this way," he continued. "There are points all over our bodies that when depressed by a knuckle or finger, cause a lot of pain. These are called pressure points. One of these areas is located just below your nose where a mustache would normally grow." To demonstrate he rolled up his sleeves, walked behind me, and wrapped his left arm around my chest. He placed the pointer finger of his right hand across my upper lip. He then exerted pressure to the area pulling upwards towards my nose.

It hurt, really hurt, in fact it brought tears to my eyes. But the pain only lasted for a moment.

With this demonstration over, my formal martial arts training was concluded as well. Apparently he felt this one move, a finger strategically placed under the nose, was all I needed to reverse my bad fortune at recess. And maybe all I needed to protect me for the rest of my life. But somehow the pressure point "secret" failed to instill the confidence I had hoped for. No added inner strength either.

I felt completely disenchanted with this training until I had an opportunity to use this new technique. Philip De Anda, my next door neighbor, and I would often wrestle in the front yard. Philip had an older brother who had taught him some real wrestling moves like head locks, scissors locks, and half-nelsons. Philip had used these on me on more than one occasion and I can't say I enjoyed being placed in any of these holds.

One day Philip had gotten me in a pretty good head lock and just about the point I would have given in, I decided to implement the pressure point strategy I'd learned. I pressed my knuckle into his rib cage as hard as I could. I was hoping to find one of the pressure points my dad had referred to in my somewhat abbreviated training. When I applied this move Philip immediately released me and cried foul. "It's not fair wrestling with you," he moaned, "you know all the pressure points!"

"All the pressure points?" I thought. I wasn't even sure I'd found one. But apparently I had. When I heard this, it occurred to me that maybe the simple technique I learned from my dad did have some value after all. I'm not one hundred percent sure it would be effective if I was attacked in a dark ally by a thug. But for a wrestling match at school with one of my fellow classmates, or with Philip on the front yard, the pressure point strategy seemed to work just fine.

In every boys life there comes a time when learning self-defense seems necessary. Maybe it's an instinctive desire as we begin to understand our environment and assess the dangers around us. When this desire surfaced in me, I'm glad I had my dad to teach me his version of self-defense. The pressure point system gave me the confidence I needed to make my way safely through life.

BLACK BEAUTY
the baseball story

I come from a baseball family. No one actually played in the big leagues but I have a cousin on my mother's side who was drafted out of high school by the St. Louis Cardinals. I'm not exactly sure what happened with his baseball career, but I hear he's now a lifeguard somewhere in the San Diego area.

In my earliest childhood memories whenever the family would get together, which was quite frequently, the main topic of conversation was always baseball. Leading the discussion was the family *Commissioner of Baseball*, my grandfather, Ed Lefebvre. As patriarch of the family he declared himself to be the leading expert on the subject. If you wanted to join the conversation you better know your stuff. Not only did he know the batting averages of just about everyone in baseball, but he also knew the finer points of the game; the rules. For twenty years he'd been an umpire in the Connie Mack League and, as a result, he knew the rule for every situation, even those as rare as a Buffalo nickel. His credentials were impeccable.

He also had a sense of humor. One time at a family gathering he posed this scenario to the group: You are the official scorekeeper and there is nobody on base. The batter hits the ball down the right field line into the corner. The fielder races to the ball, but before he gets to it, a pig jumps out of the stands, scampers onto the field and with 30,000 bewildered fans watching, eats the baseball. How would you score this?

The room fell silent as everyone considered the situation. With no one able to come up with an answer, Grandpa, with a perfectly straight face, spoke. "You'd rule it an inside the *pork* home run!"

I started playing baseball when I was about 8 years old. Most of the time we played in the empty lot behind Uncle George's duplex. We'd use pieces of cardboard for the bases and a 2 inch by 4 inch board for the pitcher's rubber. Since the lot was rectangular in shape, we'd position the batter in one of the corners and declare right field closed. During those long days of summer we'd play ball until dark. And then we'd follow my mom's rule to "come home when the street lights come on."

When I was nine I started playing organized ball. I played Little League in the Culver City American League. The fields were a far-cry from the dirt lot I'd grown accustomed to playing on. There were actually three fields in Culver City, one for the minor league teams, usually the first time players, one for the majors, usually 10 and 11 year-olds, and a larger field for the oldest kids who played in the Pony League.

Although I thought I did fairly well in tryouts I was drafted by a minor league team. I was disappointed that I didn't make the majors my first time out, but I was happy to be playing organized baseball. After all, this meant real uniforms, real rubber cleats, baseball fields with real grass and even real umpires. "This was going to be fun," I thought.

My optimism was somewhat dashed when I learned about the team I was to start my baseball career on. Unlike my friends who were drafted by teams like the Tigers, Yankees, Indians and Reds, I was picked by a new team in the league, the Seals. Ugh! What a name! There wasn't a professional team in any sport in America named after a seal. "Whose bright idea was this?" I wondered.

If the name wasn't bad enough, our uniforms compounded the problem. They were gray with orange sleeves. Perched atop our heads were black caps emblazoned with an orange "S" on the front. Splashed across the front of the jerseys, no pun intended, was black lettering outlined in pumpkin orange that shouted out our less-than-intimidating name "*Seals*."

Because of the way we looked I felt this team was doomed before we even got started. But the anticipated ribbing over the name of the team never materialized. Before long we were learning the basics of the greatest game on the planet, baseball.

In most cases kids are infielders, outfielders, or pitchers. A good coach can usually determine where a player will fit in best. Since I was better at grounders than flies, and because I didn't have much of an arm, I began my baseball career at second base. Everything hit on the ground to the right side belonged to me. This was my destiny, at least during that first year of ball.

The following year I graduated to the majors and was drafted by the Indians. Now this was a real team. I moved from second base to short stop because my arm had gotten stronger and I was getting pretty good at scooping up grounders. I now got to wear a pin-stripped uniform fashioned after a professional team, the Cleveland Indians. This was much cooler than the uniform I'd worn as a Seal. Things were starting to look up.

The baseball diamonds in Culver City were great. The ground crews, made up of player's fathers, kept the fields in tip top shape. The dark green grass was thick and weed-free. The infield dirt was dragged and raked to remove all but the tiniest pebbles before it was watered down. There were few, if any, bad hops on these fields.

Similarly the dugouts were authentic, with three steps leading down to the pine bench. Before games the field was meticulously lined with chalk to make it official. Perched behind home plate, in a booth with a view of the entire field, sat the announcer who introduced each player over the public address system.

The outfield fences consisted of brightly painted sheets of plywood 4 ft. tall by 8 ft. wide. Each panel contained the name and logo of a local business which paid a sponsorship fee. Just beyond the sign in left field was a fully operational scoreboard that kept track of runs, hits and errors. Every detail of these fields was perfect and it took Little League baseball to a higher level. It was easy to imagine how big leaguers felt when they went to work. This was serious baseball!

Like most kids my age I harbored an instinctive fear of getting hit with a baseball. You didn't have to be a brain surgeon to figure out that if you were hit with an object as hard as a rock, coming off a bat like a mortar shell out of a bazooka, you'd get hurt. The only defense you had was a small piece of leather called a glove that you'd have to strategically place between the ball and your body. And even though I tried to suppress this fear, my subconscious "will to live" kept it alive.

This fear was always magnified when standing in the batter's box. But it was worse when Skip Wright, the Senator's pitching ace, was on the mound. No one on the sandlot had ever thrown a baseball as hard as he did. And what made matters worse was the fact that he had the confidence of an executioner. When he threw the heater, the ball looked like an aspirin shot from a rifle. On top of that Skip Wright was WILD! Not exactly an attribute that would help raise *my* confidence level.

As I stood in the on-deck circle watching the big left hander finish his warm-up pitches, I had a revelation. The dictionary defines revelation as a "divine manifestation." I'm convinced that's exactly what it was.

As I studied Skip's wind-up and delivery, it occurred to me that things might not be as life threatening as I originally thought. Skip, being left handed, actually delivered the ball from an area away from me. As the ball traveled through the air it then moved toward the plate. The opposite was true for a right handed pitcher because the pitch began on my side of the plate.

In other words, with a southpaw, or lefty, the ball came from the outside in, which would theoretically reduce the risk of being hit. To me whether this concept was scientifically accurate or not wasn't important; the fact that I *believed* it was true was all that mattered. As I snapped the chin strap on my batting helmet and walked toward the plate, my confidence level miraculously soared.

I stood in the batter's box and looked out at Skip. I was calm and relaxed. I took a practice swing as he looked in for a sign from the catcher. He nodded once and went into the wind-up. The ball left his hand as I started to swing. My theory was guiding my every movement.

The ball reached the plate at the precise moment my bat was crossing it. The sweetest sound in the world, when a baseball is hit with a wooden bat at the perfect spot, resulted. *Crack* the ball exploded off the bat and projected toward left center field. This ball was going deep. The outfielders turned and ran toward the fence in a futile attempt to catch the ball. They stopped running and watched as it sailed over the sign advertising "Brill's Auto Parts." As I rounded first the umpire signaled "home run." At that moment my whole life changed.

I slowed to a jog as I touched second base, then third, and trotted to home. I had done it! I had hit my first home run! My teammates swarmed me at home plate as I was slapped on the back and butt by everyone. I sat on the bench looking out as the scorekeeper placed the run up on the board. "That was *my* run" I thought. My theory had worked and now I had the proof. I sat back on the bench, my smile never bigger.

When the game was over I stood in line at the snack bar with my fellow team mates. Every player got a free snow cone after each game. But that day, since I hit a home run, I was given a hamburger for my achievement as well. No hamburger ever tasted so good. But the best was yet to come.

A few days later I got a call from my Grandpa. This was the first time I'd ever talked to my grandfather on the phone and I felt a little strange. "Jimmy," he said in a very official sounding voice, "your mom tells me you hit one over the fence the other day. That's terrific. What are you doing Saturday morning?" "Nothing," I told him, since our game wasn't until the afternoon. "Well I want you and I to take the bus downtown to the sporting goods store. Any grandson of mine who can hit one out of the park deserves his own bat." The Commissioner had spoken. I felt like I'd been inducted into the Hall of Fame.

The bat I picked out was a Louisville Slugger, 31 ounces, painted and lacquered jet black with white grip tape. And burned into the barrel was the name "Black Beauty." It was the coolest bat in the world.

As the bus headed down Culver Blvd., it dawned on me. I'd come a long way from those days on the Seals. In the past week I'd hit my first home run and now I was sitting on a bus, next to the Commissioner of Baseball, with my very own bat between my legs. And I realized that life doesn't get any better than this.

THE BRIDGE OVER BALLONA CREEK

My love affair with Christine Johnson began and ended with a kiss — a kiss I'll never forget. For the better part of the seventh grade school year "making out" was the main topic of discussion among the guys. I imagine the girls talked about it as well. A lot of things were beginning to change for me, both internally and externally, and most of these changes had one common denominator — girls.

Only months prior to this time, I'd considered girls to be a pain in the butt. Basically they got in the way of the activities I cared most about; playing baseball, slot car racing, and one-on-one basketball. But almost overnight that changed. I found myself entranced by the wild tales of conquest other boys were eager to offer. It seemed like everyone had a story about "making out" — everyone but me. I'm not sure how, or even if Webster's Dictionary defined the term, but I understood "making out" to mean "kissing a girl on the lips for a long time." This was a bridge I hadn't yet crossed. But that was about to change. It was time and I was eager to take the plunge.

Talking about something you've never done before and actually doing it are two different things. There are a lot of factors to consider. First I needed to find a girl I liked. This wasn't that difficult since just about every girl in the seventh grade had begun to look pretty good to me. Next I had to find a girl who liked me. This was a little more challenging since most girls are somewhat shy and tend to keep their feelings inside, making it hard for guys to figure them out.

Usually you'd have to rely on a third party to pass a note or make a comment like "Judy Cavallo thinks David Warnier is cute." I didn't come across any notes or hear any rumors that contained my name and a girl's name in the same sentence. Here I was planning to embark on the most significant journey of my life without knowing exactly who my traveling companion was going to be. "This was going to be risky" I thought, and the intense fear of rejection almost derailed the entire plan.

I spent a good part of each day wondering what it would be like to actually kiss a girl. Just thinking about it made my heart race. But since I wasn't exactly skilled at conversing with girls, my chances of succeeding were low. Without a willing partner, making-out wasn't going to happen.

Then, out of nowhere, came an answer. Christine Johnson, a really cute classmate with long blonde hair, an acne free complexion, great smile, and glasses with light blue plastic frames, entered the picture. She did so by simply talking to me on several occasions. This event might not sound that important, but because I was too shy to initiate a conversation with her, her taking the first step was huge in the overall scheme of things.

Christine was perfect. And the only reason I hadn't considered her before, was because of one thing. Her only flaw, if she had one, was her height. Christine Johnson was the tallest girl in the seventh grade — maybe the tallest seventh grader in the city.

At the other end of the height spectrum was me. I was the shortest kid in the class and had been since my first day in kindergarten. I'd spent every school year, including this one, being first in line for everything because of my size. Being short was a cross I was forced to carry and standing next to Christine only made it heavier. Nevertheless, my eagerness to explore my feelings outweighed the problem with the difference in our size. After all, I was on a mission.

Christine apparently didn't own a bike, or if she did, she wasn't allowed to ride it to school. This was a problem for her because she lived a good three miles from school. But it gave me the perfect opportunity. I began by offering to carry her books while walking her part way home. The routine was simple. I'd carry her books from the school yard, walk her to the bridge over Ballona Creek — the halfway point — talk for awhile, say good-bye, and run home to arrive in time for dinner. As each day passed, we were getting more comfortable with each other and the difference in our heights was forgotten. This scenario continued for weeks. Then it happened.

One afternoon while standing on the bridge after talking for a good twenty minutes, just when I would usually pass her load of books to her, I blurted out a question. "Why don't I walk you the rest of the way home?" It was a gutsy move on my part driven, I suppose, by the subconscious activities within me. If she said "no," it would be a clear sign that the bridge over Ballona Creek was not only the half-way point home, but the end of the line for our relationship. The question hung in the air like a balloon only partly filled with helium. She stared at me, smiled nervously, and after a brief hesitation, nodded in approval.

Once over the bridge we had passed the line of demarcation. I repositioned the load of books to a fresh arm and we began the trek toward Christine's house. From that moment on I began thinking about the kiss.

As we walked…I wondered, "Was Christine thinking about the same thing I was? Was I being overly optimistic in assuming that Christine wanted to kiss me as much as I wanted to kiss her?" I waited anxiously for clues in her voice like a poker player waits for a new hand to be dealt. I was hoping that she'd bring up the subject of kissing but I realized that would have made my job too easy. Nothing Christine said or did indicated she was thinking about making-out with me. And the kiss I contemplated for months was now beginning to fade for lack of a plan.

As we approached her house, Christine casually mentioned that her mom was home. This bit of information was important. If we were going to do anything more than walk home together, privacy was paramount. Her mom being home took away our main option. Being unfamiliar with her neighborhood, I had no idea where we could go to be alone. Only Christine knew and I wasn't even sure she *wanted* to be alone with me.

I sat on the porch while she took her books inside. My arms were killing me. While I waited I tried to figure out a plan without much success. My confidence was beginning to erode. The whole idea about making-out was about to go down in flames when Christine emerged from the house. She had changed out of her plaid uniform skirt and white blouse into jeans and a T-shirt and had pulled her long blonde hair back into a ponytail. She looked terrific, but more importantly, she had a plan.

As the screen door closed behind her Christine made a suggestion. "Why don't we go behind the garage?" Bingo! The sign I was looking for. There could be no doubt that we were thinking the same thing. Her suggestion pushed my heart into high gear and I realized that today was definitely going to be my lucky day.

As we made our way around the garage a strange feeling began to churn in the pit of my stomach. It was like the feeling I had the first time I climbed the ladder up to the high-dive at the Culver Plunge. I was about to do something I'd never before attempted, and I wasn't sure if I could do it.

The area behind the garage was ideal. There was about ten feet between the garage and the back fence. It was over-run with weeds and crab grass three feet high. This was a good indication that no one had been back there for years. On the other side of the 6 ft. fence was an embankment that led up to the freeway. The constant flow of speeding cars provided a sort of background music for us. The important thing was that we were alone, at last.

After asking a few general questions about the likelihood of getting interrupted, I was convinced that this was the perfect spot. Now the hard part. The moment of truth had arrived. As I stood in front of Christine my heart raced and my hands began to tremble. I'd never been this close to a girl before, not like this anyway. I looked through the blue frames of her glasses deep into her eyes and smiled nervously. Words were unnecessary. I'd seen enough movies to know what to do next. I'd move my lips toward hers and just before they met, I'd close my eyes. I'd probably hold my breath, but I wasn't sure about that part. I'd play that by ear.

I gently put my hands on her hips, wet my lips one more time, and stepped closer to her. Just then something happened. The difference in our height suddenly became an issue. We were close enough to kiss but even though we both wanted to, we *couldn't*. Reality struck. Since she was at least a head taller than me, her lips — the most important part — were out of reach. I looked up at her and gazed into her eyes, which were even further away, and realized that desire alone wasn't going to make this kiss happen.

The anticipation that had been building for the better part of an hour, suddenly turned to panic. What in the world was I thinking about when I decided to make-out with Christine?

Again I moved my face toward hers, hoping that maybe the difference in our size was a figment of my imagination. But our second attempt was as fruitless as our first. Christine smiled nervously, obviously realizing the futility of the situation. My first kiss — a kiss I'd waited for all my life — now seemed unattainable.

In desperation my thoughts immediately flashed to Sally Black, a cute girl in my class who was actually an inch or two shorter than I was. Why hadn't I tried this with her instead of Christine? The situation seemed hopeless.

But there is something instinctive about kissing. When a boy and girl like each other something very natural and beautiful takes place. Although our first and second attempt at making contact was a disaster, the awkwardness of the moment didn't deter us.

Undaunted by our previous failed attempts we both realized another approach was needed. Christine had to bend down at the precise moment that I stood on my toes and looked up. This was our next strategy. We gave it a try and what resulted was a sort of swiping motion of her chin across my forehead. We immediately went into a hug as I placed my head on her chest and she rested her chin on top of it. We stood motionless lost in a predicament beyond our control. I was about to give up when something in the grass caught my eye.

Lying in the weeds at the base of the garage was a board about ten feet long. It was about the size and shape of a board used for a teeter-totter and was covered with various shades of paint. It apparently had been used as a scaffold the last time the house was painted. Could something as obscure as a paint splattered board buried in weeds three feet tall actually be used to salvage the moment? With my arms still wrapped around Christine's waist the plan that had previously eluded me suddenly materialized.

We stopped hugging so I could move the board into place. It was heavier than I could handle so I asked Christine for help. Together we pulled it out of the weeds and dragged it to the fence. On the count of three we lifted one end and positioned it on top of the six foot fence. The other end disappeared into the weeds against the base of the garage wall. The resulting angle of the board was perfect. This was going to work!

No instructions were needed. I straddled the inclined board with my back to the fence while Christine positioned herself a foot or so lower and faced me. Any difference in our height was neutralized by the slope of the board. I looked into Christine's eyes, which were now directly across from mine, and at her lips which were within inches. And the kiss I'd waited for all my life, unfolded. It was long and good. So long that I had to breath through my nose during it. And just like that it was over.

But getting to that point had taken time, a long time. Darkness had fallen like a pig on roller skates and now I needed to get home.

Three miles is a long way. For a kid running in the dark, it seemed like twenty. Physically exhausted but emotionally satisfied, I could barely make out the image of my dad coming towards me from the bridge over Ballona Creek. The street lights had been on for a good hour or so and that meant trouble.

I couldn't tell from his gait if he was going to hug me or kill me. He did neither. Instead he just yelled at me, inserting some descriptive words I'd never heard him use before. He said over and over that the entire family, including most of the neighbors, had been out looking for me for hours.

When he stopped yelling long enough to ask where I'd been, I told him I'd walked Christine home from school. I decided at that moment against going into the details. Shaking his head from side to side while holding up his finger as a pointer, he repeated over and over that I wasn't going to walk anyone home from now on because, as far as he was concerned, I was grounded forever.

      Later that night as I replayed the events of the day in my head, the thing that kept surfacing was the kiss. It was the most exciting and magical experience of my life until then. And even though it was the first and last time I kissed Christine, it would be the kiss I'd measure all other kisses against for a long time.

FIRST LAUNCH

Growing up is hard — especially for a kid! — and seventh grade proved to be a turning point in my life. I'd gained a lot of confidence during the previous school year and things were looking up. Life was starting to make more sense to me as well, or so I thought. It was during this time that a simple rubber band changed the balance of power in Sister Margaret Mary's class, and taught me a lesson I'll never forget.

I, like a lot of boys in my class, had a paper route. When school was out the paper boys would descend on designated street corners to fold newspapers. Bundles of papers marked with route numbers were tossed there each afternoon and we'd sort through the bundles and go to work. The tools of the trade were pretty basic; a bike, canvas saddle bags emblazoned with the name of the paper you were delivering, and rubber bands. It was easy to tell which corners served as drop points because rubber bands by the hundreds were scattered everywhere!

As we plied our trade, folding papers then securing them with rubber bands, we would often fire a rubber band or two at a fellow carrier or passing car. Shooting rubber bands was a common practice, a tradition among paper boys worldwide I imagine. But it was a practice that was not universally accepted, especially not by Sister Margaret Mary.

Shortly after the school year started I was elected class president. As chief executive officer of Sister Margaret Mary's class, I presided over class meetings and represented the class at various functions during general assemblies. I took this responsibility seriously.

At any given time during the school day, because there were so many newspaper carriers in the class, one could get hundreds of rubber bands by taking them from the pockets of the carriers. Half the class was armed to the hilt! So a rubber band hurling across the classroom was a frequent site, but was a practice Sister Margaret Mary disdained. She viewed a rubber band as a weapon, a lethal weapon, and vowed to rid the class, if not all of society, of them.

Her somewhat harsh stance on rubber bands meant two things. First, if you were going to violate her ban, good timing had to be exercised to avoid getting caught. Secondly, one had to use discretion in selecting only the most favorable targets. Shooting the wrong person — someone who would fink or tattle on you — would be tantamount to death. This was a serious undertaking.

I refrained from participating in the rubber band fights mainly because I was class president. I believed it was my responsibility to set an example for my classmates. On top of that, to reinforce her position on the subject, Sister Margaret Mary had doled out punishments for this infraction on more than one occasion.

Up to this time I'd managed to leave *my* rubber bands at home. As I sat at my desk, which was located toward the back of the room, an errant rubber band came sailing through the air and landed next to my folded hands. I glanced around to see if I could determine who the shooter might be, but there was no indication from the faces. I placed the projectile in my hand.

Looking straight ahead as Sister Margaret Mary wrote on the chalk board, I toyed with the rubber band between my fingers. I considered the options. Up until now I had refrained from this sort of activity. This was both noble and proper I thought. On the other hand, what harm could there be in shooting one rubber band, one time?

My eyes fell upon Judy Cavallo as the idea circled my head. I'm not sure why but Judy and I didn't see eye-to-eye on anything. Sitting just two rows over and a couple of seats ahead of me she was easily within range. I continued to roll the rubber band between my fingers, looked at Judy, and decided to shoot. Target selected I now had to wait for the perfect time to launch.

Within minutes Sister Margaret Mary turned to write a long sentence on the board. I loaded the warhead between my fingers, made some mental calculations regarding angle of elevation and projection, zeroed in on Judy, and fired.

The result was immediate and quite unexpected. The warhead hit Judy in the cheek and she screamed in pain. The entire class, including the nun, turned in her direction. What they saw was Judy holding her face and sobbing like she'd been shot with a .357 magnum. The nun vaulted over desks to Judy who was now *writhing* in pain. Judy's performance could have won her an Oscar.

As the nun was assessing the injury I was feeling sick. This harmless incident was taking on atomic proportions. And the fallout was just beginning to hit me.

Sister Margaret Mary spent a good five minutes comforting Judy and decided there was no need to call the paramedics. Instead she sent Judy to the restroom to freshen up and to regain her composure.

The nun now stood before us as solemn as a judge before a jury in a murder case. "I want the person who shot Judy to stand up." The word "shot" somehow sounded a little strong the way she said it; I would have preferred her to say "hit with a small rubber band," but she didn't. The class sat motionless waiting for the perpetrator to reveal himself. Wasn't there a law regarding self-incrimination? Obviously this wasn't a Hall of Justice. Holding the rubber band before her — she should have labeled it Exhibit A! — the nun repeated her request more clearly and slowly.

"Crap!" I thought. My heart was pounding and I began to sweat as I prepared for the inevitable. I was guilty of all charges and Judy's over-reaction had helped elevate the infraction to a capital offense. Before the nun could make a third request, I slid out of my desk and stood up. A collective gasp of surprise could be heard from the class. I stood before the judge, jury, and executioner, *without* a lawyer. The resulting silence was deafening.

With the entire class staring at me, Sister Margaret Mary asked me to leave the room and sit on the bench outside. Being banished to the bench was the normal punishment for most infractions in the seventh grade but up to now was an experience I'd never had.

Outside on the bench I gazed at the sea gulls eating left over lunch crumbs. In the center of the school yard the American Flag was waving in the wind and the sound of the rope that hoisted it banged out an irregular clang. I'd never seen the school yard at this time of day from this perspective. And I thought to myself that as far as punishments go, this actually wasn't that bad.

This thought didn't last long as Kenny Houle, a fellow classmate and friend, pushed open the door and announced that I could come back in. As I passed him he shook his head and whispered, "Sorry, Jimmy." I took this as an omen and prepared for the worst.

I entered the classroom and stopped at the front as the nun instructed. I stood before the class as Sister Margaret Mary read my sentence. In a voice as serious as a surgeon she said, "Jimmy, you are no longer the class president." The words cut like a scalpel. Nothing else was said. Nothing else needed to be said. The sentence was worse than death. I'd been impeached!

As I walked down the aisle to my empty desk I passed Judy who looked at me with a smirk. It's funny how quickly she returned to normal after nearly being *killed* by a rubber band!

Sitting at my desk, stripped of the presidency, I felt angry and disappointed, mostly with myself. I'd given in to temptation and now I'd paid the ultimate price, all because of a rubber band!

Several weeks later during a class meeting that was run by Mike McCormack, the class vice-president, Tommy Grabon, another friend of mine, raised his hand to be recognized. "I move we get Jimmy back as president." The motion was immediately seconded. This sentiment caught me completely off guard. But then the nun stepped in. "That issue must wait until the next class meeting in two weeks." My ordeal was coming to an end. Within two weeks I was reinstated as class president and I was back on top of the world.

Later that year President Kennedy was assassinated in Dallas. We were in the middle of a civics class when someone from the office came in with the bad news. As a group, we were shocked. Some students began crying out loud. And suddenly my problems were put into perspective.

I learned a lot about myself during my seventh grade school year. I eventually gave up my paper route and I never shot another rubber band, at least not in a classroom. But most importantly, I learned that every decision a person makes in life, whether good or bad, has consequences. Taking responsibility for those decisions is an important part of growing up.

PAPER BOY BLUES

The entrepreneurial spirit consumed me at an early age. Steve Turlo and I were always looking for ways to make money, and one of our first endeavors was the simple task of collecting soda pop bottles and cashing them in. We'd get 3 cents for a 12 ounce bottle and a nickel for a quart size. (Aluminum cans weren't invented quite yet but soda pop bottles were everywhere.) We'd pull a wagon and scour the alleys and trash cans around town for discarded bottles and would have no problem finding enough to cash in for a dollar.

From soda pop bottles we graduated to mowing lawns. Steve had the edge here, no pun intended, because he owned a lawnmower; I didn't. We'd go door to door asking people if they'd like their lawn cut, front and rear, for a buck. After a full summer of mowing lawns — and making what seemed to us like a lot of money — we were ready for real jobs. The newspaper business was our next challenge. But this endeavor lead us down slightly different paths.

For a kid with a bike a paper route was a great way to establish a regular income. You had a fixed number of customers and every day — except Sunday — you'd fold papers, load them on your bike, and throw them on porches and in driveways. But delivering newspapers on a bike wasn't the only way to turn a buck. This is where Steve and I differed.

Instead of a paper route but I chose to sell papers on a street corner; same product, different channels of distribution. While Steve had a fixed number of papers he'd toss daily, my volume would fluctuate. But selling papers on a corner had several advantages.

First, while Steve was kneeling on a corner somewhere, folding papers and loading them into his bags, I'd have already sold 15-20 papers. Then, while Steve was riding around the city throwing papers on porches and in driveways, I'd be selling more papers. You'd be surprised by how many people would buy a newspaper from a kid standing on a corner. While

Steve was out fighting traffic in the late afternoon being chased by a dog or two, I'd be on my way home with cash in my pocket.

Every 30 days Steve would have to go out collecting; every paper boy I knew couldn't wait to collect at the end of the month. That's when they got paid for a month's worth of work. It's also when they collected their tips which could make or break a kid. This system was fine for Steve and a lot of other kids but I preferred my method. There's nothing better than working and getting paid the same day, and the corner was the ideal place to accomplish this.

Just as I was getting established as the "newspaper kid on the corner" another opportunity came along. A new newspaper, the Blue Ribbon Independent, offered an entirely different distribution system and consequently a different way to make money.

The Blue Ribbon Independent was anything but a newspaper. It only came out once a week and instead of news it was filled with page after page of grocery store ads. Bundles of these were dropped off on just about every corner in the neighborhood each Thursday and left there for the taking. Thrifty housewives would walk to the corner or send their kids to pick-up a free copy of the paper.

But someone at the Blue Ribbon corporate office came up with another way to get these papers to customers. The plan worked like this. Every Thursday any kid could go to the corner, pick-up the free papers, fold them, and deliver one paper to every house on the street. Then every other month, the same kid could go to the houses he'd been delivering to for eight weeks and try to collect 80 cents. *Try* being the operative word here.

Collecting 80 cents for a paper no one actually subscribed to was going to be a challenge. So the whole idea was a risk, but risk is what business is all about. Although my previous formula for making money (selling papers on the street corner) was working, I felt the time was right to try something different.

After delivering about a hundred papers once a week for two months, I acquired a stack of official looking receipts from the Blue Ribbon, and I went around collecting. The scenario was the same. I'd knock on the door and in my cheeriest sounding voice I'd say, "Collecting for the Blue Ribbon Independent."

This statement, no matter how friendly and non-threatening it sounded, would always elicit the same response. "We don't subscribe to the Blue Ribbon Independent!" Then I'd have to explain, with the door closing in my face, that the paper is actually available for free on the corner on Thursday, but as a courtesy to them I've been delivering it to their porch. If the door wasn't entirely closed at that point, the puzzled face behind it would ask, "Why would you do that?" My next statement would seal my fate. "You don't have to pay for it if you don't want to," I'd say dejectedly. The few people who hadn't closed the door at this point would look at me and ask why I thought they should pay for a free paper they didn't subscribe to? I didn't have a good answer. After hearing the same argument about fifty times, I got to the point that even I didn't think they should pay for the stupid paper.

As you can imagine, the tips were few and far between. The only people who actually paid the 80 cents were people who really didn't understand what I was talking about and decided to pay anyway, or people who felt sorry for me. In either case what I earned was a mere pittance for the amount of energy I spent delivering the papers. For two months worth of work I'd collected $4. I strayed from the formula and paid the price.

Its conditions like these that test the spirit of the true entrepreneur. A good businessman always knows when it's time to cut his loses and walk away. So I made a business decision — I decided to quit the Blue Ribbon Independent and go back to the corner.

I learned a couple things from this experience. First, don't expect anyone to pay for something they can get for free. Most people aren't that foolish. Secondly, when you have a good thing going, like I did selling papers on the corner, stick to it. Going into a new venture that is unproven and risky may sound great, but nothing actually beats getting paid for the work you do.

THE THREE FACES OF GRANDVIEW

"Suddenly the cliff fell away. The shores sank. The trees ended…and far away, its dark head in a torn cloud, there loomed the Mountain."
The Hobbit by J.R.R Tolkien

Grandview Street was the only hill I knew of that was perfect for skateboarding. It provided a long unbroken run of sidewalk that began at the water tower at the top and got progressively steeper as it sloped to the bottom some three hundred yards away. Toward the bottom it flattened to allow the rider to coast to a gentle stop. It was steep, long, and unconquered. It represented much more than a hill. Conquering it by riding a skateboard from top to bottom became the criteria used to determine a kid's entry into manhood. It was the ultimate challenge.

A strip of grass about three feet wide ran parallel to the sidewalk between it and the street. This strip of grass provided a critical safety net for a skateboarder out of control. Diving off an errant skateboard onto the grass was the preferred alternative to the concrete; that grass saved lives!

From the top of Grandview next to the water tower one could see Catalina Island some 30 miles away. Peering down Grandview with skateboard in hand, the sidewalk seemed endless. At the top the wind blew constantly making the hill feel more like a mountain. To succeed in riding to the bottom took nerves of steel and sheer guts, a combination most kids in the 6th grade simply didn't possess.

Steve Turlo was my best friend at the time. He was a tall lanky kid with braces on his teeth and a moderate complexion problem. We affectionately called him "Bucky." Tommy Grabon, another classmate of mine, was about my size and weight and because of this we were paired whenever we had to form a line. In Catholic School this was nearly every day. Our common size became our bond.

Steve was the veteran in the group. Although he'd never made it to the bottom of Grandview he had the most attempts and held the record for making it down the farthest. I had the next most experience but still fell short of Steve's mark by a significant distance. This would be Tommy's first attempt.

To prepare for the challenge the hill presented, the three of us met at Steve's to tune-up our boards. The most important element of the skateboard were the wheels. They were secured to the axle and pivoted on a piece of rubber — a cube about an inch wide — that rested between the axle and the board. This piece of rubber was critical. It served as a shock absorber as well as a stabilizer. It was possible to adjust the axle by tightening or loosening the screw over the rubber. This would make turning easier or harder and also would determine the stability of the board.

The thought of riding the hill again awoke butterflies in my stomach. As far as we knew no one had ever made it all the way down before. To us conquering Grandview for the first time on a skateboard would be equivalent to breaking the sound barrier in a jet. Each prior attempt had resulted in disaster. No one was sure it was even possible.

Steve had managed to ride the longest and furthest before leaping to the safety of the grass. I had previously gone to a point about halfway down when my board started to violently wiggle back and forth forcing me to abort the run. As I tightened the axles I reflected on each of my previous attempts. One thing was certain; the hill would generate speeds that could only be described as blinding. I tightened the axle with all my might to make the board as stable as possible.

As we walked from Steve's house to the top of the hill, we surveyed the grass strip. We pointed out to Tommy how it could save his life in the event he went out of control. We also stressed that he would be better off jumping a little too soon rather than waiting until the board was completely out of control. A jump too late could mean missing even the grass.

We arrived at the summit with a cool breeze blowing in from the ocean. The talking ended. It was time for quiet reflection on the challenge at hand. It was us against the hill.

Bucky decided Tommy should go last. He'd need all the technical pointers he could pick up as he watched each of us disappear down the hill. Steve asked me to go first and respecting his position as veteran, I obliged.

I held the board under my foot and peered down the hill. It was like looking down an elevator shaft. I knew this ride could end my life. The longer I waited the harder my heart pounded and the more scared I became. It was now or never. I placed both feet on the board and leaned gently forward. I began to roll down Grandview and to my fate.

As the wheels rolled over the seams in the sidewalk they began sending a rhythmic signal to me. The message went through my feet up my legs and through my body. Within seconds the sound reaching my brain was a rapid staccato similar to machine gun fire. Wheels beneath me were screaming. Wind blowing in my face was causing my eyes to water. I strained to see. Everything other than the area immediately in front of my board was a blur. Blinding speed, which was Grandview's trademark, had reared its ugly head. And then it happened just as it had on so many occasions before. Despite the fact that I had used all my strength to tighten the axle before the ride, the board began to wobble. The survival alarm inside my head went off and instinct took over from there.

In a flash I found myself flying through the air toward the safety of the grass. I slid across it, arms and legs flailing, trying to stop. It was a good twenty feet later before that was possible. I had crashed but was still alive! I crawled to my feet, grass burns on my hands and elbows, and waved to the others on top of the hill, a signal that I was O.K.

By the time I had rejoined the others, Steve was ready to go. Seemingly without hesitation, he leaned forward on the board and was off. Within seconds he was barreling down the hill and fading from our sight. He passed the point where my run had ended and then past the point where he had previously jumped off his board and continued down traveling at what seemed to be the speed of light. The sound of the screaming wheels faded as the board, with Steve on top, vanished down the hill.

And just like that it was over. He leveled off toward the bottom and threw his hands into the air. We cheered wildly from the top. Steve had done the impossible. The mountain had finally been conquered!

We ran to the bottom of the hill and took turns patting him on the back. His board had held up and so had he. With this run down Grandview, he'd become a hero.

It was now Tommy's turn to take the test. Steve's advice which had now gained even more credibility was simple; stay on the board until it wobbled. If it didn't, you'd have a good chance of beating the hill.

Tommy stood motionless at the top of the hill, fear controlling his actions. He waited for his gut to tell him when to go. Several minutes passed before he finally found the courage to launch himself.

He was about a third of the way down when disaster struck. His board pitched violently from side to side and tossed him like a Brahma bull throwing its rider. He never made it to the safety of the grass. Instead he was planted, face first, on the concrete sidewalk and slid a considerable distance until he came to rest. Steve and I ran down the hill in a frantic race to aid our fallen friend — we were sure he was dead! Tommy was bleeding from his forehead, nose and chin. He was holding his shoulder as blood ran down his elbow. He was a mess, but alive.

We lifted him to his feet and assessed the damage. He was bruised and bleeding but able to walk so we helped him back to Steve's house where he called his mom to pick him up. The sight of blood was sobering. The danger that was Grandview's legacy reaffirmed itself.

Grandview had been conquered that day but then she'd gotten her revenge. While Steve had earned his place in our history book Tommy had almost gotten killed. What happened to him could just as easily have happened to me. He'd pushed himself far beyond what instinct and common sense had dictated and he paid the price.

I learned something about myself too that day. I knew that to accomplish something like riding Grandview required a lot more than sheer determination. It required a combination of practice, confidence, and luck. I hadn't been able to conquer her that day but I knew with more practice my confidence would grow and with a little luck, someday I would make my mark upon her.

THE BUICK SPECIAL

I can't eat a grilled cheese sandwich without thinking about my Uncle George. It all started when I was 13 years old. Although Uncle George had two sons of his own they were too young to be useful on this particular day. He'd phoned my mom on Friday night to see if I was available to help him on Saturday. He was moving his family from a rented duplex and to get his cleaning deposit back, the place had to be spotless. After she asked me if I'd like to give up my Saturday to help —she quickly interjected that Uncle George *really* needed me — I obliged by saying, "OK."

Uncle George had always been one of my favorite uncles. The empty lot next to his house served as the local sand lot (a baseball field) where some of the greatest games of my life took place during summer. He'd always be around to shout out encouragement and to provide the Kool-Aid after the game. So I didn't actually mind helping him clean even though it was a Saturday.

He came to pick me up around 7 a.m. The plan was that we'd work side by side using hot soapy water and sponges to wash the walls and baseboards of the vacant rooms. Uncle George used a ladder to get the areas I couldn't reach and to scrub the vents. He kept mentioning "elbow grease" which I understood to mean the grease marks on the walls left by people's elbows. Heck, there were marks all over the walls, and I suspect they were left there by more than just elbows! Regardless of how they got there, I did my best to clean them off the walls. The work was hard and dirty. By 2 p.m. we had finished washing all the walls. We were done for the day.

Just across Centinela Boulevard, about two blocks up from the freshly cleaned duplex, was a diner I'd previously seen but never entered. A wooden sign painted light blue with big dark blue letters sat on the roof that said "Gramma's Kitchen." Uncle George pulled his big old Buick into the rear parking lot and we entered the restaurant from the back. Entering the building from the rear — where the employees entered and the deliveries were made — gave me the feeling that Uncle George had been here on more than one occasion. We sat in folding chairs — the kind my mom would bring out of the closet when we had a house full of family over for Thanksgiving dinner — and leaned over the Formica topped table. Uncle George handed me one of the small red menus that were tucked between the napkin dispenser and the light blue wall. "What do ya feel like eating Jimmy?" I gazed at the entrees and not sure what to order I turned the decision back to him. "I'll have whatever you're having Uncle George."

"Two grilled cheese sandwiches and two Cokes," he told the waitress who was now standing before us. It sounded good to me. While we waited for the food to arrive we talked about the Dodgers chances of winning the World Series. Then we moved on to talking about how I was doing in Pony League.

My mom once told me that when Uncle George was a kid he'd broken his nose playing baseball. As a result his nose, which was fairly large to begin with, was pushed to the right of where it should have been. Sitting across from him eating the grilled cheese sandwich I actually had a chance to study it without making either of us feel uncomfortable. Mom was right; his nose was as crooked as a door with one hinge! But since it was that way because of a baseball injury I thought it was kind of cool. His misdirected nose was kind of a battle scar.

After we finished lunch Uncle George paid the bill and turned to me and handed me a dollar. "Thanks for the hard work," he said. I hadn't expected to be paid and told him so, but he insisted, so I put the money in my pocket. We walked to the car the same way we'd come in and headed home.

As Uncle George drove the Buick Special I noticed we were taking a different route. Instead of going straight home like I expected, he headed in the opposite direction. We were driving in an undeveloped part of the city that was actually the future site of Marina del Rey, a huge boat harbor. Vacant land seemed to stretch for miles with nothing but freshly laid roads bisecting huge lots. I peered out the window of the Buick at the various stages of the planned development as he pointed out where the channel for the harbor would be dug.

Then Uncle George did something quite unexpectedly. He pulled the car to the shoulder of the road, shifted it into park, and pulled the spring loaded hand brake. "Come on," he said, "I want *you* to drive." Before I knew what to say, he'd opened his door and was walking around to the other side, to take his place as passenger.

The closest thing to driving I'd done before to this was when I was 10 and my dad had taken me to an empty parking lot next to Douglas Aircraft. He let me sit on his lap behind the wheel of his Plymouth Belvedere steering the car as he worked the pedals. As I slid across the front seat taking my place at the helm of the Buick, something occurred to me. The Buick Special wasn't a new car but it was *his* car. And since he didn't own a home it was — without a doubt — his most valuable worldly possession. Putting it in the hands of an unlicensed 13 year-old with no driving experience was no small matter. And I understood the magnitude of this event.

I took hold of the steering wheel and peered out over the enormous hood as Uncle George explained the intricacies of the car. The Buick Special had both power steering *and* power brakes so when I was ready to stop he stressed that I needed to "go easy" on the brakes.

After providing the details required to maneuver the machine he suggested I slide the bench seat forward. Then I adjusted the rear-view and side-view mirrors. With one foot on the accelerator and the other on the brake I turned the key. The huge V-8 engine responded with a roar. I prepared for take-off.

I moved the gear shift from "P" to "D", looked over my left shoulder, signaled my intent to enter the lane by stretching my arm through the opened window, and took my foot off the brake. The car eased forward even before I pressed on the accelerator. I gently guided it away from the shoulder and into the street.

As the engine began to rev, the car drifted to the left and then the right as it responded to the gentlest of my steering commands. The car and I were communicating without words! Within minutes, with the car traveling about 25 mph, I began to settle in and to enjoy the scenery from my new perspective in the driver's seat. I was "King of the Road."

Uncle George let me drive for a good amount of time and we'd made several loops around the area. I returned the car unscathed to the point we'd started and pulled off the road, gently placing my foot on the brake as instructed. I brought the Buick to rest like a mother lays a sleeping baby into a crib. I set the shifter in "P," pulled the emergency brake toward me and shut down the engine. The experience was over.

Uncle George gave me a gift that day. What started out as giving up a Saturday to work with him, turned into an unforgettable experience. Trusting me with his Buick Special made *me* feel special. It also said that he looked at me as more than a kid. Without saying a word, Uncle George considered me a man. That was the greatest gift of all!

TABLE FOR FOUR

The most embarrassing moment of my entire life happened when I was thirteen years old. The good thing about it happening when it did was that I got it over early in my life and nothing, in over thirty five years since then, compares.

Charlie DiStefano was an only child, the son of an Italian mother and father. He was in the "other" eighth grade class and the thing we had in common was the fact the he and I were both planning on attending the seminary upon graduation from grade school. In a few months we were going to begin the long journey that would lead us to the priesthood. As a result we had a bond.

At the urging of his parents Charlie invited me to his house for dinner. I'm sure it was their idea not his because no thirteen year old kid invites someone for dinner. So I found myself on my way to Charlie's, completely unaware that in a few hours my life would be changed forever.

Before dinner Charlie and I played basketball in his driveway until it got too dark to see. Drenched in sweat, we went inside and washed up with the smell of garlic and tomato sauce filling the house. Spaghetti and meatballs, yummy!

Dinner at the DiStefano's was different than what I was used to. For one thing it was a much more formal affair. Real china instead of the melamine plates we used at home, linen napkins instead of paper, leaded crystal in place of plastic tumblers, and more eating utensils than I knew what to do with. A center piece of fresh flowers was flanked by two candles arranged on a beautifully embroidered tablecloth imported from Italy, I guessed. I'm not sure if this was the way dinner was served every night or if this was special because I was there. I sensed that this occasion called for my best manners and I was prepared to exhibit them.

Mr. DiStefano led us in prayer before dinner thanking the good Lord for the gift of this food and friends. At the conclusion Charlie's mom asked me to pass my plate to Mr. DiStefano who would be doing the serving. This seemed unusual, at my house we served ourselves. Oh well, when in Rome; do as the Romans, I thought to myself. I handed my plate to Charlie who passed it to his dad. I'd worked up an appetite playing basketball and was famished.

As Charlie and I talked I could see out of the corner of my eye that Mr. DiStefano was loading up my plate. He used the large fork to pile one scoop after another of pasta on my plate. The portion was so large that the blue pattern circling the plate's rim was completely obscured by the mountain of spaghetti which he then topped with enough sauce to paint an entire house red!

Then he handed the plate to Charlie who, using two hands, passed it to me. It must have weighed a good four pounds. At home this would have fed our family of five!

The portion was enormous. It reminded me of Mount Vesuvius and to make matters worse, the three meatballs which were resting on top were the size of baseballs. If I was expected to eat all this then I was in trouble, serious trouble. I surveyed the other plates of pasta around me, all of equal size to mine, and I before I took my first bite I began to sweat.

Outwardly I engaged in the conversation but inside I was frantic. How was I going to finish what lay before me? Was this some kind of joke? I considered my options. First, I was under no obligation to eat the entire thing. Let's face it; I didn't have any say in the amount of pasta I received so why should I feel compelled to finish it? This line of reasoning brought only momentary relief. One of my mom's favorite phrases rang through my head. "Waste not...want not, the good Lord said." Leaving anything on my plate would be more than just rude, it was bordering on sin. Not an option.

My next idea was to simply approach this like a man. I mentally divided the plate into four equal portions. I would systematically consume one section at a time, include one of the meatballs, rest for a minute or two, and continue until the task was completed. I would finish the main course and "pass" on dessert should it be offered. It sounded simple enough and I was sure it would work. This was the plan I would go with.

As the dinner wore on I forged ahead toward my goal; to eat everything on my plate. As I made my way through the spaghetti, sweat began pouring down my forehead. I twirled one load of noodles after another on my fork and into my mouth. Twirling, eating and talking...more twirling, eating and talking. My jaw was working overtime. Between each bite I inventoried my plate. Amazingly I'd cut the serving down to half with just one meatball remaining.

By this point I'd eaten more spaghetti than I had in my entire life. I was so full that I was having trouble breathing. My pulse began to race and I was sweating now the way I did playing basketball just before dinner. Despite extreme discomfort, I stayed my futile course. I was out of options — except for the obvious one which was to stop eating. But since I was more worried about what they would think of me if I did, I ruled this option out as well.

I continued to eat. And finally I placed the last forkful in my mouth. I reached for my napkin, wiped some sauce from my mouth then casually wiped the sweat now dripping from my brow hoping no one would notice. Finished, I sat back in my chair in shear agony.

Charlie was still going strong, devouring his salad which he saved for last. Crunching and chomping and crunching and chomping — he attacked the food before him with a fury. The sound of his fork tearing into his salad only made me feel worse. My stomach was beyond stuffed. I could hardly breathe. I couldn't take it anymore. Just as Mrs. DiStefano politely asked me if I'd had enough, I did the unthinkable. I barfed.

The flowers, the candles, the embroidered tablecloth, the fine china, nothing was spared. I ran from the table to the closest sanctuary, the bathroom. Once inside I knelt over the toilet but nothing happened. It was too late. I sat on the edge of the bathtub in total disbelief hoping that what just occurred might turn out to be a figment of my imagination. But it wasn't. It happened and there was no escape.

My embarrassment was total and complete. I considered climbing out the small window located above the tub and would have if there was something to stand on to reach it. The only way out was the way I'd come in and that meant facing the entire family. Facing a firing squad for a quick end would have been easier.

So I sat in the confines of the bathroom for a good thirty minutes until I heard a soft knock on the door. It was Charlie's mom who whispered through the door and asked if I was all right. I opened the door and said "yes."

As we walked down the hall, I apologized. She put her hand on my shoulder and said, "Things like that happen, don't worry about it." She said it in a way that only a mother could and it made me feel a little better.

Mr. DiStefano drove the car while Charlie and I sat in the back seat. Except for the roar of the engine, it was pretty quiet. I'd been invited to his house for dinner and I'd barfed at the table. It's that simple. It's kind of hard to ignore an event like that and even harder to develop a meaningful conversation afterwards. As a result of what had happened our friendship was never quite the same.

There comes a time in everyone's life when certain events or circumstances lead to embarrassing situations. When that happens a person needs to realize these kinds of things happen to us all. Different circumstances...same feelings. Dinner at Charlie's was the most embarrassing and humiliating moment of my life. And it made me feel horrible. But it happened a long time ago and I survived. And nothing since then has come close to being as bad. Amen.

SUMMER of '62

Every boy wants an older brother. Having two sisters, I looked to my cousin Freddie, a few years older than I was, to fill the role. Because he lived some fifty miles away, it was only during the summer that I was able to spend any quality time with him.

I once saw a movie called "Boy's Town." In the movie an older boy carried his little brother on his shoulders, for miles, in the freezing snow. When someone asked him, "Isn't he heavy?" The older boy courageously replied, "He ain't heavy...he's my brother." From the beginning I had a pretty clear idea of what a big brother was suppose to be. So I was somewhat disillusioned when during the summer of '62, while under the watchful eye of my cousin Freddie, I nearly lost my life.

Summer vacation meant time at Freddie's house in Torrance. I'd go there for two weeks, come home for a week, and go back for another two. By the time summer was over, I'd have been with Freddie more than I'd been with my family.

It didn't matter what we did when I was at his house, just being with him was fun for me. We'd play touch football in the street, baseball in the empty lot behind his house, or walk to the beach. Occasionally he'd invite his friends over and I'd get to hang out with them too. We'd stay up past midnight watching the Dick Cavet Show, eating bowls of Campbell's vegetable soup and drinking Kool Aide. I thought he was the coolest guy on the planet. Even though Freddie was just my cousin, it was easy to consider him my older brother, even though he wasn't.

But not everything at Freddie's was perfect. There was one thing I dreaded: washing and waxing his dad's Pontiac Lemans. Here it is summer, a time I waited nine long months for, and we'd spend half a day in the sizzling sun detailing a full sized Pontiac. This would kill me! We'd wash the car with soap and water, dry it, and apply hard paste wax by hand. Then we'd each take a side and buff that car until it sparkled like a diamond. Most people waxed a car like we did once or twice a year, but not Freddie. We'd labor over the car repeating this ritual every time I'd visit. The worst part was that this was always Freddie's suggestion *not* his dad's. Imagine a kid coming up with such an idea over and over again! And since I never saw a nickel for my efforts, washing and waxing the Leman's in this manner was cruel and unusual punishment.

But I endured the aggravation because I loved my cousin Freddie. He was my idol. If waxing a car repeatedly was the price I had to pay to spend time with my favorite person, I'd do it. And as a result my uncle drove the shiniest Pontiac Lemans in the City of Torrance. Not a bad deal for any of us.

Being the adventurous type, one day Freddie suggested we hike to the point of the Palos Verdes Penninsula. A trail lay at the base of the cliffs between the rocks and the Pacific Ocean. It followed the shoreline for about two miles ending at the point. The trail was several feet wide bordered by a steep wall of rock some fifty feet high on the left and the pristine blue ocean on the right. We made our way along the trail in the warm summer sun, Freddie pointing out the details of the rock formations and the various shells along the way. Meanwhile the tide slowly began to rise. We didn't realize the consequences of this until it was time to turn back and then it was too late!

Tired from the long hike to the point, with the sun beginning to set, we started our return home. The tide had risen significantly over the past hour or two and parts of the trail we'd previously followed were now being washed over by breaking waves. We needed the trail—we still had a good mile to go. But within minutes it was obliterated by the pounding surf. The setting sun took with it the warmth it had provided all afternoon. Getting cold, the trail gone, the tide still rising, and the surf rumbling at our feet, we needed to make an adjustment.

We had two choices. Continue along the trail that was all but non existent and risk being crushed between the waves and the cliff, or climb the face of the cliff and take our chances crawling along small ledges formed by cracks on its face. One was bad, the other worse! Climbing the cliffs and ledges would have been difficult for the most experienced climber with an arsenal of clamps and ropes. But the waves now slamming into the base of the cliff over the trail meant certain injury, maybe even death. We were forced to climb the face of the cliff.

We carefully ascended the jagged cliff until we were sure the waves couldn't reach us. I stayed as close to Freddie as I could, mimicking every move he made. Once we were a good distance up, we needed to move sideways. Freddie led the way and I used the same footholds in the same crevices as he did. I leaned into the cliff with my outstretched arms desperately clinging to its face. With the mounting waves crashing some thirty feet below us, we continued moving in this manner inching our way to safety.

Then it happened. With Freddie a good twenty feet ahead of me, my foot slipped and I instantly went into what I knew was a death fall. I've heard it said that the last conscious thought a person has the second before dying is deciding whether to scream or not. That's exactly what raced through my mind. Scream or not scream? Because I was with Freddie, my role model and hero, the last decision I'd make on this earth was to be brave, even in the face of death. So I decided against screaming.

As I began the plunge to the bottom, with my life flashing before me, something I'd only previously seen in a cartoon happened. My hand caught hold of a branch growing out of the side of the cliff! I clung to the life-saving shrub that held firm and supported the weight of my body. As I dangled from the branch, my brain was unable to comprehend what had happened in the previous second or two. Broken rocks and other debris fell in slow motion to the ocean below.

Adrenaline and the will to live kept me holding on for my life. I spotted a foothold that I was able to use to steady myself and I pulled myself back up on a crevice. I was trembling and shaken—who wouldn't be?—but alive.

Frozen in fear, I needed a few minutes to catch my breath. In order to move I decided I couldn't look down at what almost became my final resting place. Meanwhile Freddie, the big brother I'd always wanted, had failed to take notice of the events that almost cost me my life! He continued his crawl across the face of the rock to safety. When we both made it back to the beginning of the trail, I decided against telling him the details of my brush with death.

But a week later I would have another "date with death." Freddie and I had decided to go to the beach to spend the afternoon body surfing. The waves at Avenue I were usually pretty big but on this particular day they were accompanied by a rip current, a combination that would become my nemesis.

It's hard to stay together when you're riding different waves so Freddie and I were quickly separated by about 50 yards. Freddie, being older and stronger, was a lot better equipped to handle the situation than I was. Minutes into the water a rip current flexed its muscle and began pulling me out to sea toward the crashing waves. Within seconds I was in an area known as the "impact zone." This is where the waves break with a force strong enough to overturn a truck. As Freddie swam in a safe area, I was being pummeled by the eight foot breakers.

The crashing waves were relentless! Walls of water as tall as buildings fell on me and pushed me to the ocean floor. To make matters worse I was in a rip-current. I attempted to dive under each wave before it had a chance to break, but it was getting harder and harder to hold my breath. My lungs felt like balloons ready to burst.

With no lifeguard on duty I frantically looked for Freddie. "He ain't heavy, he's my brother!" The words replayed in my head. Now, more than ever, I needed a big brother like that and I needed him fast. I could see Freddie between swells a short distance away and I yelled to him. But my cries for help were muted by the slamming waves. One more wave holding me down would probably be the end. He was my only hope, but he was oblivious to my situation. I took another breath and desperately groped for the bottom as another wave tumbled over me. It was hopeless. The end was near.

Held under the churning salt water for the fifth time I was unable to hold the breath I desperately needed to sustain my life. Out of options I gave up struggling for my life and accepted my fate. I started saying an act of contrition..."Oh my God I am heartly sorry for having offended thee." I was about to be killed at the hands of a heartless sea, a few yards from the big brother I always wanted.

Now only seconds away from leaving this world something miraculous happened. The wave that was rumbling over me, crushing me against the ocean floor like a cigarette butt under a cowboy's boot, suddenly subsided. Within seconds, I was released from its death grip and was able to surface through the white-water.

I gasped for air expecting to see another huge wave descending upon me. But there wasn't one. The last wave that nearly finished me off was the last wave of the set. The rip current was gone as well. The sea had stopped roaring as quickly as it had started, and in its place was a lull. This was the break I needed. I spent my last ounce of energy swimming to shore where I stumbled to the safety of dry sand.

I sat in the warm sun, exhausted and dazed like a badly overmatched boxer after fifteen rounds. Just minutes earlier my life had flashed before me. And now I sat and watched Freddie ride one wave after another knowing he didn't have the faintest idea that I'd nearly perished...again.

I was beginning to realize that spending time at my cousin Freddie's this summer had an enormous price tag. In the two short weeks I'd been with him I'd come close to death twice; once by nearly falling off the face of a treacherous cliff and once at the hands of a murderous ocean.

At that moment I made a decision. It was time to return to the more familiar, if not safer, environment of my own neighborhood. Summer was just about over and I'd had enough excitement with my "big brother" Freddie to last me for a long time.

Life is a precious thing. The events over the previous weeks with my "big brother" Freddie convinced me of that. And it put things in perspective for me. In the summer of '62 I realized that having two younger sisters instead of a real big brother wasn't that bad after all.

PEOPLE ON THE PLANET

People are everywhere, and where there are people, there are stories. The people who were part of my life became part of my stories. Some were there only briefly — a short chapter in a long book — others were there for the duration. But regardless of the time, each left their own mark in a unique and personal way and helped define me as a person.

Most were unaware of what they meant to me and since some are gone forever, they may never know. But to each of them I am indebted, for they enriched my life by their presence, their love, and their example. I'm glad we were on this planet at the same time; they helped make the journey interesting.

Here are a few glimpses of the people I remember best.

The Gift of Music

Miss Reynolds was my Kindergarten teacher. She did a great job of managing a classroom full of runny-nosed, sometimes high-strung, five and six year olds. She taught us nursery rhymes, the primary colors and our numbers. She introduced us to the messy skill of finger painting and then taught us the fine art of cleaning up afterwards. She read us stories with a voice as soft as a pair of flannel pajamas. And through it all she made each of us feel special.

The one thing that made Miss Reynolds special was something she did every afternoon. After we'd all eaten a hearty lunch and run around the playground like wild animals for awhile, we'd come inside for a rest. Exhausted, we'd file into the classroom, make the mandatory stop in the restroom, and go to the cubby marked with our name and grab our neatly rolled blankets.

We knew the routine. We'd make our way to the area in the middle of the classroom and spread out the blankets. After everyone was settled on the floor Miss Reynolds would bring her chair and sit among us. It was then that she'd bring out her violin and begin to play.

Lying down on the blanket, my face warmed by the sun piercing through the south facing windows, I could smell the hardwood floor beneath me. I'd close my eyes as the collective sound of our breathing deepened and slowed. All activity ceased except for the sounds cascading from her violin. Like a gentle breeze pushing a cluster of small sailboats across a lake, her music gently guided us as we drifted to sleep. This was nap-time, and the music created by Miss Reynolds made it magical. It was a teacher's unique gift to her students. Long after those days of innocence were gone, the memory of the music Miss Reynolds created remains.

A Welcome Visitor

He'd come to our house once a month to collect the rent — ninety dollars for the two bedroom one bath unit we called home. My mom would keep an envelope marked "rent" in her dresser and when he came, she'd disappear temporarily into the bedroom to retrieve it.

Mr. Calhoun was our landlord. He owned the duplex we occupied for a good many years when I was growing up in Culver City. When he came every month, my two sisters and I would sit at the kitchen table and he'd engage us in conversation, asking each of us how we were doing in school. Mom would return and hand him the envelope. He'd take the envelope, fold it in half without counting the contents, and put in his back pocket. He'd finish the conversation with us and then reach into his front pocket, take out three silver dollars, and hand one to each of us kids. With that, he'd thank my mom, tell us he'd see us next month, and he'd be gone.

He wasn't in our house but five minutes a month. I never knew where he lived, if he was married, had kids or anything else about Mr. Calhoun. All I know is that he came to our house each month, collected the rent, and gave us something back. What a cool thing to do. In his own way Mr. Calhoun was making the world a better place.

After forty years, I still have every silver dollar Mr. Calhoun gave me when I was a kid. The memory of his kindness still shines as bright as the coins he gave me.

The Gatekeeper

They were in their late sixties, retired from another line of work I imagine, good neighbors and good people. They were also my first employers.

Mr. and Mrs. Stebbins lived in the pink house next door to us. It was the corner house on the block and the couple operated a small business in it. It was a pottery shop — Stebbins' Pottery Shop. They'd added a large room to their house and it became the showroom for knick-knacks, gardening supplies and other items.

Outside on the lawn was an array of stone fountains and clay pots, bird baths, statuary, pink plastic flamingos and green frogs made of cement— everything you needed to make your garden unique. The entire collection was enclosed by a chain link fence to keep vandals out and, according to Mr. Stebbins, "To keep the artificial wildlife from escaping!"

One Saturday just before closing, Mr. Stebbins came over to my house and asked if I'd like to help rearrange a few of the pots in the yard. I'm not sure what prompted this request. Maybe he was getting a little tired because of his age and needed the help of a strong young kid. Whatever the reason, I agreed to help.

Some of the statuary had been knocked over during the course of the day and I'd set them back up. I'd reposition the plastic flamingos and rearranged the cement frogs. After that I'd go into the store and sweep the floor while Mrs. Stebbins counted the till. After about 45 minutes I'd be finished and Mr. Stebbins and I would close the door to the shop and then we'd close the gate outside. He'd hand me the padlock and key. I'd open the lock, slide it through the hasp, and secure the store for the day.

This was an important job. Holding the lock and key to another man's business meant that I was trusted. It was a responsibility I took seriously. After I closed the lock— tugging on it twice to make sure it was secured—I handed him the key. He'd reach into his pocket and hand me a quarter in return. My job was done. And working for Mr. Stebbins at his pottery shop, even though I was only nine, made me feel important.

A Long Walk Home

Sometimes you can learn more from a stranger in five minutes than you can from someone you've known forever. We lived in a duplex located on Sawtelle Boulevard, a street with a constant flow of cars whizzing by. This wasn't exactly the kind of street you could play a game of baseball on. Because it didn't have a signal or stop sign on it, just getting across it was a challenge for a kid. Too big a challenge my dad had determined, so we had a rule in the family. None of us kids were allowed to cross the street unless one of our parents helped us.

After visiting my friend David, who lived across the street, I'd have to stand directly in front of my house and yell over the traffic as loud as I could, until my mom would come out and cross me. Sometimes this took forever. But the rule was a good one, because none of kids ever got hit by a car.

One afternoon while playing in the front yard, I noticed the city bus stop on the other side of the street. After a minute or so the accordion doors closed, the air brakes shooshed, the big diesel engine roared, and the bus pulled away. Left behind was a woman. I didn't actually know this lady but I knew she lived across the street about seven or eight houses up from where I lived. She was middle aged, short and heavy, with long black hair streaked with gray and pulled back and wrapped in some kind of netting. She always wore a black overcoat no matter what time of the year it was. Her shoes were the kind the nuns wore, black heavy-duty lace-ups with a wide heel, built to support a train. She usually carried a cloth sack filled with groceries and secured on the handle of one of her crutches tucked under her arms.

As she made her way up the street, relying on the crutches for support, she swayed from side to side. The added weight of the grocery sack made the going difficult, her progress slow and cumbersome. But she forged ahead the best she could.

I called to my mom and asked her to cross me over. The lady was no more than a couple of houses closer to home when I offered to carry her bag. She appeared a little startled but her smile of approval told me she welcomed the help.

As we walked side by side, I wanted to say something to her—anything— but I wasn't sure how to start the conversation. After all she was an adult, an adult with crutches, and I was just a kid, we didn't exactly have a whole lot in common. I was relieved when she broke the silence. "Are you the boy who lives across the street?" "Yes," I replied. "I thought so." There was another long uncomfortable pause before she continued. "How do you like living on such a busy street?" Being a kid, I'd seldom been asked a question that concerned my opinion. And since I sensed she was really interested in my answer, I gave the answer some thought before replying. "Well it's not the kind of street you can play a game of football on," I commented. "But I'm pretty used to it." Another pause and then I asked, "What about you, how do you like it?" I noticed she was getting short of breath and beginning to sweat. The effort of walking this far wearing a heavy coat was now taking its toll. "I'm lucky to live on such a busy street," she said between huffs. "Busy streets have busses running on them, and someone like me needs a bus to go places."

From my perspective the busy street was a nuisance. Heck I couldn't even cross it alone! But she looked at it differently. It provided her something she needed; access to a bus. Same street, different views. And then it occurred to me, that two people living on the same street could actually be miles apart in how they looked at things.

As we slowly made our way up the street the difference between our lives was clear. The short easy walk for me was a difficult task for her. And the busy street I was forced to tolerate was actually something she liked.

Arriving at her house she climbed the steps leading to the porch and pulled the screen door open catching it with a crutch. She reached into the deep pocket of her coat and took out her keys. Pushing open the door, she asked me to put the groceries on the kitchen table. As I did, she reached back into her overcoat and took out a coin purse. She asked me to hold out my hand as she emptied the contents into it. My protest fell on deaf ears as she closed my hand over the coins and thanked me again for the help. I looked at the lady before me and I felt like I'd known her all my life. I smiled, waved goodbye, and ran down the steps. "Be careful crossing the street," she said, as the screen door closed behind me.

Twice the Fun

People always had trouble telling them apart. Although they weren't identical twins, they dressed alike and looked enough alike to fool most everyone outside of our immediate family. But even though they looked alike they were as different as two sides of a coin. Char was as comfortable climbing a tree as Sandy was hosting a tea party for her dolls. I hung around with Char most of the time and wasn't too sure what Sandy did.

One Sunday when we were returning from a visit to my cousin Freddie's house, we stopped at a park somewhere in Lawndale. My dad sat in the car, as he often did, reading a book while mom sat on a bench and watched us kids play. We took turns playing on the slides and swings and then we climbed a jungle gym that had a fireman's pole to slide down on. Everything was going great until Sandy tried the fireman's pole.

A certain amount of hand strength was needed to slide down the pole to prevent one from free-falling. Sandy didn't have the required strength and as a result, she discovered the consequences. A falling object reaches terminal velocity in a short period of time. In Sandy's case it was less than two seconds, Crack! I heard the sound of her leg breaking upon impact.

Within seconds my mom was at her side carrying her to the bench comforting her as Sandy screamed in pain. I ran to the car to get my dad and within minutes, we were on our way to a hospital just down the road.

The treatment room at the hospital was filled with stainless steel fixtures and bright lights. Because the hospital was small and there weren't a lot of patients, the doctor setting Sandy's leg left the door open. Standing in the hallway outside, Char and I could see the doctor putting Sandy's leg in a cast.

Because the three of us kids were close, Char and I felt Sandy's pain. But what could we do to help? In times of crisis people fall back on their religion for strength. Instinctively, Char and I decided to pray. I suggested saying the rosary, I would lead, Char would respond. We paced the hallway praying as Sandy lay a few feet away being tended to by the doctor.

Then it happened. While Char and I were reciting the litany of prayers— prayers to help our fallen sibling—Sandy blurted it out. "Why couldn't this have happened to Jimmy or Charlene!" Like two birds hit by the same shotgun blast Char and I were stunned. We stopped praying and looked at each other. After a long pause I said, "Sandy must really be in a lot of pain, because she's delirious!" Although I wasn't really sure what that meant. Char nodded in agreement and we resumed praying.

Several hours later we all arrived home and from that moment on the "Reign of Sandy" began. Because of her ordeal, Sandy ruled the house from her place on the sofa and spent the next 8 weeks playing with dolls, eating ice cream, watching television, and allowing the endless flow of visitors to sign her cast. I don't doubt that she was uncomfortable and needed the attention. I tell this story only to illustrate that Sandy wasn't anything like Charlene. And growing up with twins made life twice as much fun.

A Man for all Seasons

My dad was everything a good father should be; hardworking, reliable, a role model, and an active participant in our nurturing. And there was never any rest for him, basically because he wouldn't say "no" to his kids. As soon as we were finished with dinner, we'd go out front and play catch until it was too dark to see.

Sometimes he'd take us to the park and hit Char and I fly balls while Sandy played on the swings. After we'd been run ragged chasing balls he'd hit a mile high, we'd head for home but only after stopping at Frosty Freeze for marshmallow sundaes and flying saucers. My dad had a way of turning an ordinary weekday into something special for us kids. Life was sweet for a kid like me.

Nobody loved movies more than my dad and his favorite kind were musicals. During the summer he'd take the entire family every Thursday to the Baldwin Theater where we'd all get in for $1.50. By the time I was ten, I'd seen every musical ever made and knew every word to every song.

Dad was brave. He enlisted in the Army because Pearl Harbor was bombed and worked his way up the ranks to become a Staff Sergeant. Then, when most men were celebrating the end of their duty, he re-enlisted in the Navy. He was assigned to a cruiser, which is the name of a pretty large ship that accompanied aircraft carriers. He worked aboard ship as a Lab Technician and his tour of duty took him to the

Pacific and instilled in him a love of the ocean and the Navy. So much so that he considered making the Navy a career.

But instead he decided to settle down and start a family. He went to work for an aircraft company in Southern California and that's where he decided to stay. He often supplemented his paycheck with a second job to make ends meet and wouldn't allow mom to go outside the home to work. He was a good provider and a good man, and he set a good example for us kids.

But the quality I admired most about my dad was his generosity. St. Gerard Majella's Church was only a block from where we lived and my dad and I would often make a visit on Saturday afternoon. We'd kneel side by side in the deserted church praying. The hum of the constant traffic outside was muted by the heavy doors behind us. Except for the occasional creaking of the pews we were kneeling on, the church was quiet. Dad was comfortable there and as a result so was I.

After a few minutes of quality time praying, dad would signal he was ready to go by making the sign of the cross. We'd walk to the rear of the church where a heavy brass box hung on the wall just inside the doorway; I knew this to be the "poor box." And before leaving the church my dad would reach into his wallet, remove several dollars, fold them, and slip them into the box. "Now don't say anything to your mom about this, O.K. Jimmy?" he commanded. I'd nod and we'd walk home.

My dad was a good man with a good heart and he knew what was important in life. There was never time for hobbies like golf or playing poker with the boys. He gave him time to his wife and three kids. His family came first. It's that simple.

His generosity and selflessness are his legacy. And he showed each of us kids how to be a good parent and a good person.

Being There

A mother's job is never easy. My mom raised three children in a time when it was common for mothers to be at home while the dads went to work. She was a good cook, a good seamstress, making a lot of our clothes and mending everything that needed repair. She made braided rugs and curtains, pot holders and aprons, and everything in between. "Simplicity" patterns for making dresses and blouses were stashed everywhere in our house. And pinking shears, a kind of jagged edged pair of scissors, were among the tools she used to make things for us.

Her specialty was baking and her chocolate chip cookies were her signature creation. But she didn't stop there. Banana nut bread and homemade apple pie, cakes and turnovers, and cinnamon rolls were regular creations she made from scratch. Is there anything in the world better than the aroma of homemade bread? It filled our house on a regular basis.

One day my mom baked a dozen biscuits. Like bees to honey, my two sisters and I were drawn to the kitchen. As the biscuits cooled, we patiently sat at the table with a stick of butter and a jar of grape jelly. When mom gave the O.K. we polished off the entire dozen before dad got home. When he opened the door the great smell of baked bread engulfed him, but he was about an hour too late. Biscuits and butter were gone.

My mom was a magician when it came to budgeting money. My dad made $90 a week and mom had to make it last. We always had everything we needed to be safe, warm, and well fed. We even managed to take three trips all the way across country from California to Massachusetts, twice by car and once by train. I still can't figure out how she managed to save enough to do that.

We often rode the bus to Culver Center, a place with a lot of stores. It's where my mom bought me my first real leather baseball glove at the Thrifty Drug Store — all of my previous gloves were made of plastic. This is the same store that had an end display of marbles.

"All you can hold in one hand — for a dime," the sign above them read. Mom gave me the go-ahead sign and I scooped up about twenty or so in my right hand. Waiting for the cashier, the marbles fell through my fingers like sand. The harder I squeezed the faster they fell. When I finally handed the cashier my dime, I was able to put three marbles in the bag. Not a good deal for a dime.

My mom was great at being a mom but she was also a great friend. I've heard that mom's aren't suppose to be friends, that it somehow interferes with their ability to be an effective parent. But I disagree. She knew when I needed a mom and she knew when being a friend was more important. When I spent my allowance early in the week and needed a quarter for a movie on Saturday, the "mom" in her would tell me that I needed to budget my money more wisely, but the "friend" in her slipped me the money anyway so I wouldn't miss out on some fun. That's what I mean, she did both equally well.

Beyond all the material things she gave us was the greatest gift of all; her presence. She never had anything to do that was more important than being there for us kids.

I had friends who had a lot of really cool things: bikes, clothes, and cash. But these were replacements for their parents. It's easy for a parent to do that. What's not easy is making the commitment to being there. The greatest gift a parent can give a child is simply the gift of self. There is no substitute. My mom gave us that gift and the resulting sense of security was priceless. She made the journey called "growing up" fun.

THE JOURNEY BEGINS

I honestly can't remember when, or even if, I consciously made the decision. But ever since the third grade, a recurring voice inside of me kept drawing me to an idea. I know it sounds crazy because most kids, if asked about their "career plans," would offer things like becoming a policeman, fireman, or professional baseball player. But those avenues failed to capture my interest as a career. The job I wanted— the path I was drawn to—was to become a priest.

With the seed germinating inside me, my mom cultivated this idea in an indirect way. She had always sent donations to the Colombian Missions and as a result, our house received the steady flow of magazines and newsletters they'd send.

I read every story and looked at every picture they contained. The images of missionary priests working with natives in remote regions of the world fascinated me. People living in dire poverty being fed, clothed, and taught by the Columbian Fathers drew me to want to do the same thing.

My first step toward fulfilling this dream was becoming an altar boy. In addition to serving mass whenever I could, I'd go to the church on Saturdays and stock the pews with envelopes and pencils for the Sunday offerings. Occasionally I'd climb the steps to the pulpit, look out over the empty church, and imagine I was delivering a sermon to a church filled with people. I was as comfortable in this environment as most kids were at the bowling alley.

During my eighth grade school year Father Thomas, a priest in charge of the altar servers, started a contest. Since it was pretty common for an altar boy to miss his scheduled assignment, Father Thomas decided to add some incentive for any trained server who would come forward and fill in. Each time a kid filled in, he'd get a "credit." The server with the most credits at the end of the school year would get a prize at the altar boy picnic.

The challenge was laid. I loved to serve mass and since I lived a block away from church, I knew I could win this contest.

One Sunday, I served the 8 a.m. mass. After the mass I hung around for the 9 a.m. in hopes they would need a server and I could get a credit. They did and I was there to assist. I got another credit at the 10:15 mass and again at 12 o'clock mass when one of the servers failed to show. That evening at the 5 p.m. devotions, I found myself on the altar again replacing another absent server. I got four credits in one day and was well on my way to winning the contest.

By the time the picnic rolled around I had accumulated 120 credits! I won the contest but more importantly, I was paving the road to the priesthood.

The decision to enter the seminary after eighth grade was an easy one. The priesthood was my destiny and the seminary was the avenue I needed to take. I had been planning for this all of my life. There was only one problem. When I made the official announcement that I wanted to be a *missionary* priest, like the ones in the magazines I'd been reading about for years, I got some unexpected resistance from my parents. Although they wanted me to follow my dream, they were both pretty insistent about me being a parish priest versus a missionary priest. As much as they wanted a priest in the family, neither of them wanted to see their only son killed, bible in hand, in a jungle in Manchuria.

We discussed the issue at length, and I agreed to enter the seminary to become a Diocesan, or parish priest. Answering a call and serving God was the important thing and I was convinced that I didn't necessarily have to go to a remote area of the world to do this.

I'd spent the last thirteen years learning about life, and I'd met a lot of interesting people along the way. I'd made some good friends, discovered how to make a dollar or two, even had a girlfriend—well sort of—and was beginning to see how life works. I'd even managed to survive Catholic grade school. But I knew, deep within my soul, it was time to focus on my future. I was about to take the first step toward fulfilling my destiny.

While Steve and my other friends took the placement tests for high school, I traveled to the San Fernando Valley, some 40 miles away, to take the entrance exam to Our Lady Queen of Angels Seminary. Once accepted, I'd be leaving my friends and family behind to embark on a new life. I was a little scared, but not afraid. It was time to answer the knock at the door.

In the fall of 1964, just before I turned 14 years old, I entered the seminary and began a journey that would change me forever. But that's a story for another time....